BEYOND THE LAUGHING SKY

a novel

MICHELLE CUEVAS

illustrated by JULIE MORSTAD

PUFFIN BOOKS

PUFFIN BOOKS
An imprint of Penguin Random House LLC
375 Hudson Street
New York, New York 10014

First published in the United States of America by Dial Books for Young Readers,
an imprint of Penguin Random House LLC, 2014
Published by Puffin Books, an imprint of Penguin Random House LLC, 2015

THE LIBRARY OF CONGRESS HAS CATALOGED THE DIAL EDITION AS FOLLOWS:
Cuevas, Michelle.
Beyond the laughing sky / by Michelle Cuevas.
pages cm
Summary: Hatched from an egg and raised by a loving family, ten-year-old
Nashville is more bird than human except for his lack of wings, but he and
his classmates learn that differences need not keep them apart.
ISBN 978-0-8037-3867-6 (hardcover)
[1. Belonging (Social psychology)—Fiction. 2. Individuality—Fiction.
3. Self-acceptance—Fiction. 4. Family life—Fiction. 5. Orphans—Fiction.
6. Transformation—Fiction.] I. Title.
PZ7.C89268Bey 2014   [Fic]—dc23   2013034416

Puffin Books ISBN 978-0-14-242305-9

Printed in the United States of America

1 3 5 7 9 10 8 6 4 2

THE FIRST DAY OF SCHOOL

"Big day tomorrow," said Nashville's mother. Nashville tried to ignore this, and concentrated on scooping some seeds out of a bird feeder and onto his plate.

"Are you excited?" she asked.

"I am," said Junebug. "I want to get new pencils and notebooks and erasers and a lunch box . . ."

"You know," Nashville interrupted. "I've been thinking. I'm not sure I *need* any more education."

His father peered over the morning newspaper at his son.

"Maybe I could set up shop and be a traveling balloon salesman," said Nashville. "Or a skywriting poet."

His father resumed reading the paper.

"A one-man band?" continued Nashville. "A flea circus trainer?"

"Very funny," said his mother, ruffling Nashville's feathers. "Now hurry up and get dressed. We've got a busy day of errands to run before you start school."

"A cootie cleaner?" Nashville continued, his voice fading as his mother pushed him toward his room. "A star counter? A palm reader? A decoder of alphabet soup?"

OTHER BOOKS YOU MAY ENJOY

FOR MY LITTLE BROTHER, CHRISTOPHER,
WHO TOLD ME THE ENDING

—M.C.

BEYOND THE
LAUGHING SKY

IN A PECAN TREE

NASHVILLE AND HIS FAMILY LIVED IN A HOUSE perched in the branches of the largest pecan tree in the village of Goosepimple. The tree grew on the top of a high hill, and the hill overlooked the small, perfect village, where the sun always shined, the grass was always mowed, and the men strutted like doves in their gray suits.

The house in the pecan tree, however, was often shrouded in fog like the purple-gray gloom of an aged bruise, causing the old men in town to sit on their porches, drink sweet tea, and gossip.

"That tree on the hill looks like the last feather to be plucked from the pimpled skin of a goose."

"Naw, it looks like the last sprig of hair on an ancient bald head."

"Naw, it looks like the last white ghost seed waiting to fly away from a dandelion."

Tourists often wanted to drive up the one creeping road that led to the top and visit the house, but once they got close realized they had somewhere else to be or something else to do. When they stopped by the town visitor center they would say, "That house in that tree is not like the rest. Was it built there? Was it built like a nest?"

"Oh no, sugar," the old widow working at the visitor center would say. "That house sat on a small street in town for nearly a century. Then, ten years ago, there was a flood the likes of which this area had never seen. It started raining as hard as it could in March, and it didn't stop until June. Can you imagine that?" The widow paused, allowing the visitors to imagine that amount of precipitation. "Needless to say," she continued, "the rivers and swamps and the bayou overflowed. The foundation of the building came loose and the whole place just floated away, bobbing on the water like a toy in the tub. The water rose all the way over that hill, and when the rain stopped, the house was stuck in that pecan tree like a mouse in a hawk's claw."

"Who lives there now?" asked the tourist.

"A sweet young couple and their little girl," replied the widow.

"How precious."

"And also . . ." the widow paused. "And, well, that *boy*."

"What boy?"

"What boy, indeed," replied the widow. "What boy hatches from an egg?"

"Oh, fiddlesticks," a Southern gentleman said to the widow. "A boy can't hatch from an egg. That's impossible"

"What an absurd little word," the widow replied.

"Pardon?"

"You said impossible," the widow pointed out. "There's no such thing. There's things you've seen and things you may not have, but there ain't nothing that's impossible, sugar."

NASHVILLE

IMPOSSIBLE. IMPROBABLE. INCONCEIVABLE. IF the children from far-flung villages who came to catch a glimpse of Nashville had better vocabularies, perhaps these are words they would have used. As it stood, they would ride their bikes to the base of the hill after sunset, their brakes screeching like the call of a night bird, with hopes of seeing something they called just plain *weird*.

"I double-dog super dare you to go up and knock on the door and get a look at him."

And then they'd look and look at the house without moving, their hearts pounding like hoofbeats. They'd imagine they saw a light come on, or a curtain billow out like it had bones.

"I saw him!" they would shout to the wind, pedaling fast. "He's half boy, half bird!"

Had Nashville heard their words it wouldn't have mattered, for he really did look how they said—why, the truth of the matter was, he looked like a bird in almost every way. He was the size of a normal boy, perhaps a tad small for his age, but he had feathers for hair and a beak for his nose and mouth. His eyes were sharp and golden and his legs too long and thin. But when it came to clothing, Nashville was fond of bow ties and hats, and this made him about as alarming as a puppy in a paisley suit. He was, however, extraordinary, and that tended to scare townsfolk, who were hooked on the Ordinary with a capital O, and preferred their day-to-day served without any Extra.

Nashville was one of a kind, and he had a way of stirring up whispers in town, causing the old women to sit in the beauty parlor, get their hair curled, and gossip.

"That youngster looks like a dodo bird in a dinner

jacket. What's next? Turtles in tuxedos? Skunks in swimsuits?"

"I'm just glad he doesn't have wings."

"Oh! Can you imagine that? Some whippersnapper flying around, peeping in our windows."

It was true. The only avian attribute Nashville seemed to be missing, much to his disappointment, was a pair of wings. But he had everything else. Why, by the time he was a baby barely out of the egg, Nashville was not only looking like a bird, but acting like one, too—chirping instead of crying for food, preferring sunflower seeds to milk, and only settling down to sleep in the bed his parents had custom made just for him, the one carpenters had been consulted and hired to build. Branches had been soaked, bent, and twisted. The nest was as large as a bed, and made up with pillows and a soft blanket.

"Did you make your nest?" his mother asked Nashville every morning.

"And Junebug," she asked his little sister. "Did you make your bed as well?"

"I want to sleep in a nest, *too*," whined Junebug, with the misguided jealousy of a younger sibling. She was only eight, but Junebug often seemed older and wiser, and Nashville enjoyed her company. And so, from time to time, Nashville would allow his sister, Junebug, to sleep with him in his boy-sized nest.

Sometimes, especially when he was alone, Nashville would stand for a long time at his bedroom window. The interior of the house glowed green due to all the leaves outside, and was like being in the cabin of a ship that sank in an algae pond. Sometimes Nashville felt as if his soul was waiting just under the surface of his skin, ready to leap like a fish into the cool, crisp air above.

But no. Nashville couldn't fly, that was for certain, so there was no reason for his strange desire to leap. Plus, he loved living in a pecan tree. When it was windy, the branches around the house danced and made shadow puppets on the walls. When the birds sang, he and Junebug imagined that from the outside, it must seem like the tree itself was singing.

"If a tree could sing," asked Junebug, "what do you think it would sing about?"

"I suppose," replied Nashville, "it would depend on the tree. A tree starts as a sapling. If it's lucky—if it's not mowed or mocked, chewed or chopped—the tree sets roots. The tree grows branches. The tree sprouts leaves. And every part, down to the smallest speck of bark and the tiniest vein of a leaf, is shaped by the world—the particular world around the tree. One less storm, one more insatiable caterpillar, any twist or turn along the way, and the tree would be changed. The tree would have a different song to sing."

Junebug thought deeply about this. "I wonder," she said finally, "what those pines at the edge of town sing about."

"Junebug," said Nashville. "You know I've never been past those pines."

"Yeah. Me neither," said Junebug. She looked at Nashville who was staring into the distance.

"Nashville?" she continued. "I think I'd like to stay here in our tree for always. Wouldn't you?"

"Of course," Nashville replied, with only the slightest hint of doubt. "I'd like to stay here forever, too." Anything else seemed, well, downright Impossible, Improbable, and Inconceivable.

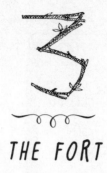

THE FORT

THE BIRDHOUSE HANGING IN THE PECAN tree was shaped like any other. It had a slanted roof, a hole for an opening, and a peg of wood that served as a front porch. The one difference was the size of this birdhouse—it was big enough for two children, and inside, instead of a nest and eggs, were books, crayons, and one small record player.

The birdhouse hung from a giant rope in the midst of leaves and was only accessible by climbing up through the branches of the pecan tree. No one was brave enough

to do this—no one but Nashville and Junebug, that is, for this was their fort.

The fort.

Sometimes, it was just a tree house. But most times it was a ship-like flying contraption with newspaper sails and oars dripping in ink. Junebug would sit in the crow's nest, binoculars to her eyes, looking out for monsters in need of a good slaying. Nashville would, of course, man the wheel. His duties also included waving to pirate kings and throwing the occasional coin to a troll when they'd cross a bridge.

The fort.

Where the pair stored their painted scenes and books of made-up languages, their two-man band, and the tiny matchbox bed plus accessories that they made in case, someday, their experiments in the world of shrinking finally panned out.

The fort.

Where once, on a most heroic adventure, Nashville and Junebug finally traveled all the way to the edge of the map, where the paper was faded yellow and thin.

"What now?" asked Junebug.

So Nashville turned over the page, and there he drew them a new map. They were travelers. They were adventurers. They were treading real dust and pebbles on the surface of an imaginary moon.

HONEYSUCKLE

JUNEBUG AND NASHVILLE WEREN'T ALLOWED to start having adventures first thing in the morning. First things first, the pair had to do their chores. And the start of the day meant taking any trash down the hill and bringing the mail back up.

Most houses in Goosepimple had a trash can on the curb and a mailbox at the end of the drive. This would have also been the case with the house in the pecan tree, except the road that wound up the hill was steep and twisted, and both the mail truck and trash truck couldn't make the trip.

"Truck's too big," explained the trash man.

"Truck's too small," explained the mailman.

"Well then, why don't you walk?" asked Junebug.

To this, neither answered, only laughed loudly.

On the trash and mail mornings, Nashville and Junebug would decide their mission on the way down the hill.

"Okay," said Junebug. "This trash is just a cover. We're picking up a top-secret encoded message in that mailbox. The mailman . . ."

"Is a *spy*," finished Nashville.

"Dum, dum, DUM!" sang Junebug.

They dumped a trash bag in the can, then crept up to the mailbox, looking around to make sure nobody was watching.

"Coast is clear," whispered Nashville.

And so they opened the mailbox. Inside were three envelopes and a coupon flyer for the Goosepimple Grocery. One of the letters was addressed to their parents from Goosepimple Middle School. Nashville suspected he knew the contents, so that one he put back inside the box.

"Come on," he said to Junebug. "I know the secret mission."

The missions were always changing—sometimes collecting jars of rain, paper bags of hiccups, adopting lost moonbeams and folding them into cake batter. Or perhaps investigating glittering slug trails left in the moonlight, finding the owners of abandoned buttons, or playing the sousaphone for caterpillars still in their cocoons.

Today, however, the mission was all about honey.

The honey was trapped inside the honeysuckle flowers, and the honeysuckle flowers were trapped on the other side of their neighbor's wooden fence. The neighbor—who had obviously built a high fence to keep out secret agents—was clearly planning a Goosepimple takeover.

"The honey," said Nashville, "can give you powers. Like invisibility. Or X-ray vision. Or . . ."

"Or it can make you fly," said Junebug, giving her brother a knowing look. Every time they went on a mission, it always seemed to end in Nashville finding, gaining, or otherwise procuring the ability to fly.

Nashville, Junebug thought, didn't seem to need the honeysuckle though. He seemed to be changing all on his own. And she would know. They spent so much time together, and she was so used to their two-headed shadow, that when she saw her own shadow it looked rather strange. But lately, Nashville had been spending time alone. Lately he'd been going for long walks, coming back with his pockets full of feathers he'd collected. Lately she'd find him standing in the yard, looking up, up, up at the sky. He seemed to be stuck in that mysterious morning place—half asleep, half awake, still able to recall a dream.

"Come on," said Nashville, interrupting Junebug's thoughts. "The honeysuckle is through the secret door."

The pair wiggled a board in the fence, loose like Junebug's front tooth, and slipped inside their neighbor's unruly garden. There were bushes growing wild, piles of leaves, and rusty, overturned lawn furniture in the yard. But there, at the far end, almost hidden, was the honeysuckle bush. Its yellow-orange blossoms drew Junebug and Nashville like bees to the flower.

"Remember how I showed you," said Nashville. He

plucked a flower, held the whole blossom in his hands, and turned it upside down.

"First pull off the bottom." He did this, and a silken string emerged from where he separated this piece from the flower. A drop of nectar appeared at the bottom.

"And then . . ." But before he could finish, Junebug swooped in and licked away the honey-tasting treat.

"Then you steal it!" said Junebug.

"Thief," laughed Nashville, and they began collecting more blossoms until they heard a screen door slam behind them and the sound of boy's voice.

"Hey!" he shouted. "My mama said to use my BB gun if I caught you in our yard again!"

Nashville and Junebug looked at each another, then started to run. They made it to the fence, and turned back as they crept through. The boy stood on his porch, arms crossed, no BB gun in sight.

"The honey worked!" cried Junebug, laughing as they ran. "I have X-ray vision! I saw his underpants!"

They collapsed, laughing, their backs against the old, tall fence. They held their hands open, and pulled the flowers apart to get to the honey-like drops hidden inside. Maybe, thought Junebug. Maybe the honey has another power. Yes, she felt sure it could transport her back here any time she had it—to a place that tasted like summer, to a place where two little shadows blended into one.

THE WELCOME CAKE

M OST EVENINGS NASHVILLE AND JUNEBUG baked a cake.

"What's the occasion?" their mother would ask. And of course, they always had an answer; they baked cakes to welcome the first firefly of the season, and cakes to commiserate incurable hiccups. Cakes for well-shaped clouds, cakes for bad hair days, and cakes only to be eaten barefoot in the grass.

"And of course," Nashville explained, "when all else

fails, there are three hundred and sixty-four days of non-birthdays to celebrate each year."

And why was Nashville so interested in cakes? Well, a cake had played an instrumental role in his fate. It's where his life story started. Well, sort of, for it most likely started when the eggs fell to the ground. Or when they were laid. Or, for that matter, when the nest was built in the first place.

Ten years earlier Nashville's mother and father had just been married, and moved into a house with a dazzling, oversized window in a small village called Goosepimple.

It was agreed by all who lived there that Goosepimple was quite simple and quite perfect. The old men sat on the porches drinking sweet tea, the dewy glasses dripping polka dots onto their trousers. Roosters perched on the fence with the red sails on their heads waving in the wind, their eyes dreaming of the sea-blue sky. Pollen-drunk bees hovered around the honeysuckle bushes. The small town held few surprises, and nothing ever changed; time circled like a bug on a glass rim, always returning to where it began.

Then one morning, surprisingly, something *did* change.

A bird—a Nashville warbler to be exact—had started to build a nest in the tree outside Nashville's parents' window. Every few minutes it flew away and returned with a new building block: moss, grass, a twist tie off a bread bag, a long strand of hair. Nashville's mother secretly hoped the hair was hers.

When the bird laid her two eggs, Nashville's mother used paint samples to identify their colors. "Pale cornflower blue," she said, holding up the paint swatch, "with a hint of mint and moss green. And the blotchy spots were a mix of rust and mahogany." She sang to the eggs as well. Nashville's mother had a voice like footsteps in new winter snow. Some say the birds in Goosepimple sang differently after they heard her. Some say they were never the same.

The Goosepimple Library had four books about Nashville warblers, and Nashville's mother checked them all out. She learned that the eggs would hatch two weeks after being laid. When two weeks passed and there were no chicks, she decided to throw them a welcome party. Perhaps it would coax them out.

"Excuse me?" her husband asked. "You're throwing a party for *whom*?"

"The birds," his wife clucked, wiping flour onto her apron. "The birds will be born any day now."

She worked extra hard on the cake. When the two large sheets of chocolate were ready, she gently removed them from the pans and used a sharp knife to cut them into the shape of a bird's profile. Her fingers turned blue mashing berries to color the whipped cream. She spent over thirty minutes drawing the feathers, eyes, and beak with the frosting bag. The cake was perfect.

"Warblers aren't blue, dear," said her husband.

"I know that," said his wife. "But I don't know how to make gray frosting."

Nashville's mother smiled. She smiled the smile of someone who believes a cake can change your fate. She smiled that smile until the morning the eggs disappeared.

"Oh my, oh no!" she cried. She stuck her head out the window and looked at the branches. The eggs and bird were gone. "The eggs," she wept. "What happened to the eggs?"

Her husband did not know. The only thing left in the tree was the nest, surrounded by small white flowers. This made his wife unbearably sad. She went into the kitchen and slid the giant bird-shaped cake into the garbage pail.

A cake. What else has the magic to turn eggs, flour, and sugar into a wish? And a cake never shows up on a bad day; never rings on a humdrum Tuesday to say, "Tough luck. You didn't make the team." No, a cake is there when things are super, when they're better-than-great—always the guest of honor at a birthday or a wedding, always dressed in frosting and wearing its boogie shoes.

Which is why it made her husband heartsick to see the cake his wife had worked so hard to make smeared down the trash bag. Is there anything sadder than untouched joy in the garbage? Her husband did not think so, which is why he immediately took the trash out to the curb.

And there, on the sidewalk in front of the house, was a broken egg.

The egg was open with chipped, white edges. Was there anything sadder than an unhatched egg? Her husband did not think so.

But where was the other egg?

"There you are," said the husband. The egg had rolled off the sidewalk and under the honeysuckle bush. This egg, much like the other, was cracked open. However, what spilled out was not a bird and it was not dead. The man lifted the creature into his hands and pulled the chips of white and blue shell from its face and eyelids. He smoothed the yellow fluid from its hair and across the crease of its mouth.

"Dear," said her husband when he re-entered the house. "I found the eggs. They were cracked on the side-walk."

"Oh no, no, no," the wife cried. "Are they dead?"

"Not this one," said the man, handing her the crea-ture.

"Why," she whispered. "This is a baby."

And it was. Inside the cracked egg the man had found

a perfect human baby. It was small—as small as a baby chick—but healthy and peach-colored and perfect.

"We'll name him Nashville," said the new mother, as if it were the most natural thing in the world to find a baby in a cornflower blue egg on the sidewalk. "I just wish," she sighed, "that I hadn't thrown out his welcome cake."

THE BIRDBATH

EACH NIGHT, ONCE THE CAKE WAS OUT OF the oven, the bakers both covered in flour and frosting, Nashville and Junebug were sent to take their baths.

"I want to take my bath like Nashville," Junebug pouted. For while Junebug took her nightly bath in a claw-foot tub, Nashville bathed each evening by moonlight in a birdbath in the yard.

Nashville slipped on his striped bathrobe, tied the belt around his waist, and walked to the yard carrying his soap and shampoo and comb. The yard was dark, but Nashville's father had thoughtfully installed a lamp for the evenings when the moon was new. This night, however, the moon was full to the brim, and washed the yard in light.

The birdbath was shaped like any other, only person-size, and to get inside Nashville had to climb a ladder. Once he reached the top, he would take his toiletries from his pocket, lay them out on the edge of the bath, and step into the water. Fed by a hose and heated all day by the sun, the water now reflected the moon.

"Scrubbing behind my ears with moonlight and sunlight in the water, both at once," Nashville liked to say.

After he cleaned his face and feathers with a washcloth, Nashville enjoyed the warm breeze and listened to the odes of insects and the limericks of frogs.

At first Nashville's father had been against the birdbath.

"He can take a bath in the tub like a normal boy," he'd said.

"But he's not a normal boy," his mother had replied. "He's special. Let's just do this one thing," she continued, "to make him feel at home."

Of course, making someone *feel* at home means making where they live feel like their real home. Which was hard, because his parents didn't really know what kind of home Nashville would have lived in had they not found him beneath the honeysuckle bush.

And neither did Nashville. Though sometimes, especially during his baths in the sky, he thought he knew. He thought he could remember coming from a place where everything could fly. A place where a clock's minute and hour hands spread away from its face, flapping like wings. A place where he'd pluck a daisy and watch the petals whirl like the propellers of a helicopter. Where he'd throw a handful of sand, and the grains would buzz away like a swarm of gnats. Where colorful fruits on a tree would burst into flight, and new ones would perch in their place.

"Anything can fly, I think," said Nashville to the pecan tree. "Dandelion seeds can fly. So can whirligig seeds. Why, just yesterday I saw a group of dead leaves fly from a tree and land on a pond. They floated away across the surface like a fleet of ships, the wind tearing at their sails."

THE TOAST & JAM
TRAPEZE TROUPE

NASHVILLE SPENT A LOT OF TIME ALONE IN the fort, since it was where he did some of his best thinking. Sometimes he'd do it lying inside, the spot of light from the door like a full moon on the floor. And sometimes he'd think while sitting on the wooden peg, the rope above creaking like a weather vane changing direction.

On a morning in September, Nashville thought about the fact that it was autumn, and that meant he was starting middle school. Which meant a new building, with new students and new teachers. Nashville was no fool. He knew the kids at his old school didn't refrain from calling him a beast or a monster because they liked him; they had just become accustomed over time to the way he looked. He also understood that it's a rare child who *wants* to go to school, but it was perhaps equally rare to dread the event as much as the tender hearts, old souls, and uniquely shaped of the world.

He was not afraid of the classes or the teachers— adults had a way of ignoring his looks in an effort to appear bravely polite. But children were not always so timid. From what he'd seen in the town of Goosepimple, one child might be a little taller, one a little plumper, but really, they looked just like one another. The same freckles, the same grass-stained knees, and the same chewed nails. *What exactly*, wondered Nashville when he saw them, *went so very wrong with me?*

As he pondered this, he heard the tin can scrape across the floor of the fort, and then the tiny voice of Junebug.

"Earth to Bird. Do you read me?" Nashville picked up the can and pulled the string tight.

"I read you, Little Bug."

Junebug spoke into her can in the house. "I have a telegram from kitchen headquarters. Breakfast is ready. Over and out."

By the time Nashville reached the table, everyone was already seated in their perch swings. The swings hung from the ceiling at the perfect height for the table, and made the whole family look like the Toast & Jam Trapeze Troupe. Nashville imagined his family in spandex and sequins, juggling muffins, balancing glasses of fresh-squeezed juice on their noses. He saw his family doing somersault flips, catching one another by gripping on to outstretched cereal spoons.

"Please pass the sugar," said Junebug, taking her seat, pouring milk on her cereal. Nashville climbed up onto his perch as well. The seats had, of course, been his mother's idea, installed to make Nashville more comfortable, and everyone—even Nashville's father, who had fallen out a few times trying to read the paper—had learned to live with, and even like, the arrangement.

"Big day tomorrow," said Nashville's mother. Nashville tried to ignore this, and concentrated on scooping some seeds out of a bird feeder and onto his plate.

"Are you excited?" she asked.

"I am," said Junebug. "I want to get new pencils and notebooks and erasers and a lunch box . . ."

"You know," Nashville interrupted. "I've been thinking. I'm not sure I *need* any more education."

His father peered over the morning newspaper at his son.

"Maybe I could set up shop and be a traveling balloon salesman," said Nashville. "Or a skywriting poet."

His father resumed reading the paper.

"A one-man band?" continued Nashville. "A flea circus trainer?"

"Very funny," said his mother, ruffling Nashville's feathers. "Now hurry up and get dressed. We've got a busy day of errands to run before you start school."

"A cootie cleaner?" Nashville continued, his voice fading as his mother pushed him toward his room. "A star counter? A palm reader? A decoder of alphabet soup?"

NOTHING TO BE FIXED

NASHVILLE, DRESSED IN HIS SUMMER SUIT and hat, set out for town accompanied by his mother, Junebug, and a warm breeze. The family marched together down the winding road, the one that circled the hill like a long, twisted strand of a peeled apple.

"Good morning, Goosepimple," greeted Nashville when they reached the village. Goosepimple was so tiny it was often forgotten on maps, so overlooked that people only seemed to end up there by accident. The village reminded Nashville of an old neighbor forever napping on their porch. But sometimes the neighbor would startle awake, almost knocking over their rocking chair. Sometimes, that is, someone new would catch sight of Nashville for the first time.

Once it had been an out-of-town aunt on a visit. She'd nearly fainted when she saw Nashville, and promptly called the police.

"We're sorry, ma'am," replied dispatch. "But we don't respond to cases of bizarre-feathered boys. Nor do we show up for curiously beaked youngsters or peculiar-shaped lads."

Nashville had made babies cry and dogs bark. He'd made at least two elderly in-laws on a visit get their glasses checked. And to top it all off, there was the issue of the ice-cream truck.

"But *why?*" Protested Junebug on the hottest days each summer, days when the sidewalk sizzled and the pecan tree tried to hunch over into its own shade. "Why does the ice-cream truck go up every street but ours?"

"Who can say," replied her mother, who suspected the snub had more than a little to do with her bizarrely feathered, curiously beaked, peculiarly shaped son.

When they reached the center of the village, Nashville and his family went to the doctor's office for Junebug's yearly checkup. In the waiting room a curious girl stared wide-eyed at Nashville. She looked at his feathers, and she looked at his beak. She looked until she finally had the courage to ask.

"So," she said. "Whatta you got?"

Nashville looked around. He put down the *Audubon* magazine he'd been reading.

"Pardon?" he replied to the girl.

"I mean," continued the girl. "What's the matter with you? Why do you look like that?"

"Nothing's the matter with him," interrupted Junebug. "What's the matter with *you*?"

"Fell off my bike," said the girl, holding up her arm in a cast. She turned back to Nashville. "You think the doctor will be able to fix whatever you've got?"

"I told you," said Junebug. "There's nothing to be fixed." She had just balled her tiny hand into a fist when the nurse emerged and called out her name. The girl's mother pulled her daughter a few seats closer, in the opposite direction from Nashville.

Nashville had been a patient at this same office for exactly one day of his life. Ten years earlier, the day he hatched from an egg, his parents had attempted to take him to this regular doctor.

"I . . . I'm not sure I'm the right doctor for this, er, specific case," the physician had stuttered. He tapped at the newborn's feathers, shined his headlamp at Nashville's beak.

"Well, where exactly do you recommend we go?" asked Nashville's mother.

And that's how Nashville ended up at Dr. Larkin's office, the veterinarian down the street—a veterinarian who, as luck would have it, specialized in ornithology and the general care of birds.

The day of his birth, Dr. Larkin put Nashville's baby X-ray up on the wall and flipped on the light. He studied it, the bones white in the dark like a bleached shipwreck beneath the sea.

"Seems healthy to me," the doctor had said that day.

"But he has feathers," replied Nashville's father. "Can it be fixed?"

"Nothing to be fixed," said the doctor. "Some children

have freckles. Some have interesting birthmarks. Nashville happens to have feathers."

"Feathers . . ." said Nashville's father shaking his head, his face still wearing a troubled look.

"So he's healthy?" asked his mother.

"Well, there is this one thing," said the doctor. "Nothing to be alarmed about." He pointed to newborn Nashville's X-ray on the wall.

"See here," said the doctor, pointing to Nashville's shoulders. There seems to be a little extra something." The doctor picked up another X-ray and put it against the light. This X-ray had the unmistakable shape of a bird's wing.

"A wing?" asked Nashville's father.

"Where a bird's wing attaches to the body, it attaches by the same joint that we see here in Nashville." Nashville's mother and father stared in silence, and soon the quiet filled up every part of the room. Why, all the cotton balls in the doctor's glass jar were simply puffed to the poof with silence.

"Are you saying," sputtered his father, "that our son is going to grow wings? That's impossible."

Dr. Larkin smiled and clicked off the light to the X-rays. "Oh, no, no, I think not. But that would be something wouldn't it? Hoo-ee. A boy with wings." He paused in thought, breathed on his stethoscope, and then wiped it like he was shining an apple. "But in the end," he said, smiling, "who can say? I know I for one try my best to never use the word *impossible*."

HAVE YOU EVER SEEN A PLATYPUS?

AND SO, AFTER JUNEBUG'S CHECKUP AT THE doctor, the family made their way down the street for Nashville's checkup with Dr. Larkin, Goosepimple's finest veterinarian.

"Well hello, Nashville," said Dr. Larkin when he walked into the checkup room. "You're growing like a weed."

"Speaking of growing," said Nashville. "Will you be taking an X-ray today, like you did last time I was here?"

"Yes, yes, first let me have a look at you," said the doctor. He turned on his light and looked in Nashville's ears and eyes and beak. He breathed on his stethoscope and directed Nashville to take several deep breaths. He tapped Nashville's knees and watched his legs kick forward.

"Now can you take the X-ray? I can't see back there too well," Nashville explained. "And you're the expert."

"Okay, okay," said the doctor. "Let's have a look."

The veterinary assistant came then and took Nashville into the room next door for an X-ray. After that, Nashville sat patiently waiting for the results. A few minutes later, Doctor Larkin returned, put the X-ray on the wall, and turned on the light that lit it from behind.

"Things look about the same to me," said Dr. Larkin.

"I see," said Nashville. He stared at the X-ray. "But what about the bone? The one that would connect them if I were to grow wings?"

The doctor looked at Nashville. He turned off the light on the wall and the X-ray disappeared.

"Nashville," he asked softly. "May I ask you, why do you want to grow wings?"

"Well, why else would I be this way?" replied Nashville.

The doctor spoke carefully and kindly.

"Nashville, you have an amazing imagination. Truly. And I don't want to disappoint you, but . . ."

"What's the point of being the way I am," Nashville interrupted. "if I'm never going to have wings?"

"Now, now," said the doctor. "None of that." He waved his hands, and the rain clouds that had started to gather in the office dispersed. "Don't waste time wishing to be something other than what you are."

"What am I?" replied Nashville. "When the world made me, it made a mistake."

"A mistake," said the doctor, rubbing his chin. "Every year the leaves change colors and drop to the ground, right?"

"Right," said Nashville.

"Is that a mistake?"

"No," replied Nashville. "That's just fall."

"Well, what about wrinkled elephants? And artichokes?" asked the doctor. "And blowfish and purple sunsets and frill-necked lizards? And platypuses! Have you ever seen a platypus? Hoo-ee. What about spiderwebs and eclipses and star-nosed moles? Are those mistakes?"

"I don't think so," said Nashville.

"Not one thing this world makes is a mistake," continued the doctor. "Including you."

"Including me," repeated Nashville, his voice sounding less than convinced.

"Why yes," said the doctor, tussling the feathers atop Nashville's head. "Especially you."

THE FIRST DAY

THE NEXT DAY WHEN MORNING BROKE, Nashville could no longer deny it: School was starting. And while he had tried to store up as much summer as he could, it was just no use. At some point during the night, summer had left town, had packed a suitcase full of fireflies and swimming holes, and whistled on down the road. And so, as Junebug raced around the house, Nashville dragged his knapsack down the stairs one at a time. *Plunk. Plunk. Plop.* He conducted the sound track to his middle school life.

"Hello," said Nashville's teacher, Miss Starling. She

wrote her name in large, loopy letters on the chalkboard. Behind it, Nashville could see the faint ghostly outline of past lessons erased from the board.

"And welcome," continued Miss Starling kindly. "I know most of you don't know one another, coming together from several elementary schools. We have lots to talk about for the new school year, but first things first. I'd like to play a game." The students tittered with excitement.

"Everyone put your chairs in a circle," directed Miss Starling.

There was much scraping and giggling while the students moved their seats. When they were finished, Miss Starling took a chair to the center of the circle and sat.

"My name," she said, "is Miss Starling. And I like sweet tea. Anyone else who likes sweet tea, please stand up."

Six students, including Nashville, stood.

"Now," continued Miss Starling. "If you're standing, quickly switch seats!"

The standing students scrambled to switch seats, but Miss Starling had sat in one of the open chairs, and a red-haired girl was left standing.

"What do I do?" she asked, embarrassed.

"You sit in the middle," said Miss Starling. "And tell us a fact about yourself."

The girl did as she was told.

"My name is Abigail. And I have a little brother."

Only two other students stood this time, and Abigail stole one of their seats. This went on for some time, and Nashville, being quite quick, avoided the hot seat. That is, until a large boy in the middle chair said, "I have a tree fort."

Nashville was the only person to stand, so he and the boy simply switched chairs. Nashville reluctantly made his way to the center, his shoes squeaking on the freshly waxed floor. All eyes were on him, and Nashville wasn't sure what to do with his face. He smiled, a bit too forcefully, and was fairly certain he must look crazy.

"So," said Miss Starling. "What is a fact about you?"

Nashville thought for a moment how to answer.

"My parents," he finally said, "were Nashville warblers."

The class snickered and muffled laughter. Nobody stood.

"Perhaps another fun fact for us, Nashville?"

Nashville thought some more.

"I was hatched from an egg," he stated.

The class had stopped tittering with laughter, and now just stared.

"I sleep in a nest," he continued.

"I bathe in a birdbath."

"I . . . I . . ." he paused, and then quickly proclaimed a final fact.

"I wish I could fly."

The students looked around at one another. Slowly, cautiously, one girl rose, then a second boy, followed by a third. Soon, the entire class was standing. Even Miss Starling rose to her feet. Nashville stood as well, and they all laughed as they bumped and bustled to take one another's seats.

SUPERNOVA

SCIENCE WAS A SUBJECT THAT NASHVILLE never quite grasped.

On the one hand, it was full of things he was intrigued by, things like how to tell the age of a tree, the dances of the moon and tides, and the names of the clouds—like cumulonimbus and nimbostratus—that sounded like magic spells on his tongue.

But science was also full of facts and truths, full of order, genus, and species, where his little life didn't seem to fit. He thumbed through the pages of his science text.

Chapter One: The Solar System

Chapter Six: Water and Weather

Chapter Ten: Earthquakes and Volcanoes

But where was the chapter on being born from an egg? About walking, and talking, but also having feathers? None of that, he knew, would be covered in this text. Or any other.

As he thumbed through the book, Nashville heard whispers to his left. A pair of girls, both larger and older looking than Nashville, whispered loudly enough for him to hear.

"If I looked like that," said the first, "I'd just want to die." She emphasized this last word dramatically like an actress.

The second girl did not answer, only elbowed her friend, and stared at Nashville. He quickly looked away.

"Do you girls have something to share?" asked Miss Starling.

The pair froze.

"No, ma'am," they answered in unison.

Nashville let out the breath he'd been holding, relieved.

"Well then, why don't you read the next paragraph," continued Miss Starling. And so one of the girls—the dramatic one, noted Nashville—began reading in her actress voice.

"'Change is the nature of nature,'" she read. "'For example, stars expand as they grow older. They grow from a star, to a red super-giant, to a supernova. When a massive star explodes at the end of its life, the explosion dispenses different elements—helium, carbon, oxygen, iron, nickel—across the universe, scattering stardust. That stardust now makes up the planets, including ours.'"

"So a star had to die to make us?" Nashville slapped a hand over his mouth. He'd forgotten to raise his hand.

"Yes, Nashville," smiled Miss Starling.

"So we're made of stars?" he asked.

"We were once stars," she answered. "Things are always changing, from one thing to another. And it can happen just like that." Miss Starling snapped her fingers.

"Some magnolias," she continued, "they grow to be trees, but then they can take up to twenty years to blossom. After decades, a silent shift, and one morning *POOF!* The flower is open, bigger than my hand."

Miss Starling closed her book, stood thoughtfully at the front of the room. "Slow, fast, in a minute or a decade. Things are always changing. From a seed to a magnolia, from pollen to honey, from an egg"—she paused, only for a second—"From an egg to a bird. There are no rules. And sometimes there are even miracles."

Nashville looked down at his own hands. He imagined a magnolia blossom twice the size. To his left, he once again heard hushed whispers.

"Like I said," said the girl. "If I looked like that, I'd just want to die."

There was a pause. The second girl tilted her head, considering Nashville.

"I wouldn't," she finally replied.

Her words, thought Nashville, sounded exactly like something made of stars.

HATCHDAY

Happy Hatchday to You.
Happy Hatchday to You.
Happy Hatchday, Dear Nashville,
Happy Hatchday to You!

THE NEXT MORNING WAS NASHVILLE'S birthday, so when his family finished singing, he blew out the ten candles (plus one for good luck) on his sesame-seed cake, wondering the whole time what could be in the big box wrapped in polka-dot paper.

"For you," said his mother, placing the gift in front of Nashville. It was too small for a hot-air balloon, a hang glider, or several of the other things Nashville secretly hoped for. Much too small for a rocket. Perhaps a hero's cape? Perhaps a telescope to see the places he longed to travel?

"Open it!" shouted Junebug, dancing around Nashville's chair, licking frosting off his candles.

When Nashville pulled the lid off the box there was, indeed, something inside that could soar through the air with ease. Its wings were silver, striped with red, and its nose came to a dashing point.

"A plane," said Nashville.

"A remote-control plane," added his father proudly.

Nashville carefully lifted the toy into his hands and turned it over and over. He lifted it to eye level and stared at it head-on. He liked the way it looked, shiny and sleek, but his first thought about it—*it's too small for me to fly in*—was just too strange for him to say out loud.

"I saw it and thought of you," continued his father. "Remember how we used to make paper airplanes for hours when you were small?"

"I remember," said Nashville. He did recall folding the paper over and over, experimenting with interior creases and wing-stabilizing folds. But mostly he remembered sailing the planes out the window. He remembered imagining a small, small version of himself sitting in the paper crease, and all the places he could go—between the boughs of pine trees, under bridges, in one window of the house, then out the other side.

"Come on," said Junebug, grabbing the remote for the plane. "Let's try it."

And so the entire family left the house in the pecan tree, stood on the ground, and stared up at the sky. Nashville's father showed him how to use the simple remote and, sure enough, when he pressed the lever forward, the plane wheeled across the grass then buzzed off into the air. Just like a fledgling from the nest, it took a few moments for Nashville and the plane to get their bearings—the wings tipped from side to side like the wooden balances above a marionette, and the nose jumped forward in jerks and sputters. But soon enough, Nashville was making the plane do loop-de-loops and zipping over his sister's head until she shrieked with delight.

"You're a natural," said his father proudly.

Even after his parents had gone inside to clean up

after the party, even after his sister had yawned her way to bed, Nashville stayed out flying his plane around the yard. He zipped it around fireflies like stars in space, and was having a wonderful time.

And yet . . .

Something was still missing. Controlling the plane, Nashville couldn't help but feel what a conductor must feel using a baton to direct a symphony. But Nashville didn't want to *conduct* the music. Nashville wanted to *be* the music. He wanted to tap-dance across the notes of the page, to visit each black circle on the sheet music like a hummingbird visits each flower. He wanted to *fly*.

Then, suddenly, the hummingbirds stopped humming, the instruments stopped playing, and the audience looked up and gasped. The small plane was hurling toward the ground.

"But how . . . ?" Nashville could only stare. For there was not one plane, but two—two planes, two comets plummeting to the earth.

A DEAD BIRD

THE SMALL BIRD LAY ON THE GROUND BESIDE the broken wings of the plane.

The plane Nashville had been flying.

The plane that had hit—and killed—the bird.

The contrast between the beautiful bird and the sad, hard ground was striking. Nashville looked closer. He saw the kind of beauty yellow flowers have growing over a carpet of dead leaves. The beauty of cracks forming a mosaic in a dry riverbed, of emerald-green algae at the base of a seawall, of a broken shard from a blue bottle. The beauty of a window smudged with tiny prints. The beauty of wild weeds.

"I'm sorry," Nashville said to the bird. His plane had struck the small thing, and now it would never open its eyes again.

"I'm sorry," Nashville said again as he lifted the bird into his hands. He touched the head and it seemed too fragile to exist, not much different from an eggshell.

"I need a small box," Nashville told his mother when he came inside the house. "A fancy one."

His mother rummaged in the closet and found a gold box, probably from the holidays. She handed it to Nashville without any questions.

"Have fun," she said. Nashville left the room. There would be nothing fun about burying a dead bird.

He went into the living room and, after making sure the coast was clear, unzipped a throw pillow on the sofa, and stole some of the soft stuffing inside. He used this to line the box, then went outside to the spot he'd left the bird under the edge of the magnolia bush. He picked some magnolia blossoms, and put the white petals in the box as well.

"I'm sorry," whispered Nashville, and lifted the bird to place her in the box. Perhaps this third sorry worked some magic, because just as Nashville said it, just as his eyes were filling over with tears, the small creature in his hands began to stir. Just a small turn of the head, and a move of the foot, but it shocked Nashville out of his sadness.

"You're alive!" Nashville shouted. It was as if the leaves of fall had flown back up to the tree, or a dead flower had picked up her petals and pinned them back on. Nashville carefully placed the bird inside the box, now an ambulance rather than a coffin, and began to run down the hill to Goosepimple.

"Back so soon?" said Dr. Larkin when he saw Nashville. The doctor had been packing up the veterinary office to head home, and Nashville caught him coming out the door.

"Please," Nashville said quickly. His hands trembled as he held out the box. "Please. I hit it with a plane and it landed in a magnolia bush and I thought it was dead but it's not and—"

"Slow down, Nashville, slow down," said the doctor leading him into the examination room.

"Hmm," said the doctor. He put on rubber gloves, lifted the bird carefully, and laid her on the table under a bright light. Nashville stood back a bit, suddenly remembering to breathe.

"No bleeding," said the doctor. "Heart rate seems good. Although . . ."

"Although?" said Nashville alarmed.

"She has a broken wing," explained the doctor. He exhibited this to Nashville by extending the wing. Instead of folding back tidily as it usually would, the wing dropped on the table, the feathers strangely bent.

"Nothing life threatening," continued the doctor. "I'll bandage it, but I should tell you, it's unlikely she'll ever use that wing again."

Nashville stared at the bird, his guilt overcoming him once more, but infinitely stronger this time.

"Without wings she can't fly," he said.

"No," said the doctor. "Like so many other things in this world, this bird will have to make do with life on the ground."

MAGNOLIA

And so Magnolia the bird recuperated in Nashville's fort. Magnolia—so named for two reasons: one, because of the bush she'd landed in, the one that had likely saved her life. And two, because Miss Starling had said some magnolias rest a long time, then bloom overnight. Nashville hoped a miracle like that for the bird's broken wing.

"Magnolia," Nashville would ask in the morning, "what would you like for breakfast?" He'd bring her seeds and nuts. Once he'd brought her a caterpillar he'd found in the yard, but she didn't seem all that interested.

Perhaps they were old friends, thought Nashville.

He would sit with Magnolia on the edge of the bird-house, beyond which only winged-things could go. He greeted the other birds that came to visit his patient, and nodded his head, even though he didn't understand a chirp of what they were saying. It was probably just gossip anyhow, news about worm delicacies and the new hot-spot bird feeder down the street.

"I wish I could understand you," Nashville would tell Magnolia when they were alone. But like the needle-point puzzles of spiders, or the language left in leaves by beetles, Nashville could not decipher a word.

When he wasn't with the bird, Nashville worked with his father, fixing the broken plane.

"A little glue," said his father. "A little Styrofoam, a little wood, almost like new."

"Can't wait to fly it," Nashville lied. He took the plane back to his room and hid it away in the toy chest. He didn't want Magnolia to see the plane and suffer any post-traumatic stress. Nashville couldn't bear to fly it anyhow. He already had one bird injury on his con-science, and no interest in another.

The plane had, however, given him an interesting idea.

"What do you think?" he asked Magnolia. He held up a sketch on paper.

"See here," explained Nashville. "I could *build* you a new wing."

The bird turned her head to one side. Then the other. She looked at the pencil sketch of a wing with feathers sewn onto it, along with a leather strap. She looked from every angle just to be sure she understood the plan.

"I'll take that as a yes," said Nashville. And so he went to work shaping the frame of light wood and Styrofoam left over from the great plane rebuilding. He recruited Junebug to collect feathers outside.

"For what?" she asked.

"No questions," answered Nashville. "But I'll give you a penny per feather."

"Make it a nickel," said Junebug, walking out the door to hunt for fallen feathers.

Magnolia had been recuperating for several weeks in the fort, and it had been near impossible to keep it from Junebug. Nashville wasn't even sure why he was—maybe a mixture of guilt and wanting the bird all to himself.

After Junebug returned with a handful of feathers, and left with a pocketful of nickels, Nashville did the hardest work of all—hand sewing each feather onto the leather wing he'd cut out while she was gone. It was a challenge, and he had to use all his books and knowledge of which type of feathers went where, and how each played a special role in lifting and soaring and gliding on the wind. However, it was all worth it, for when he had finished, the wing was truly a work of art.

Nashville placed the small wing on the floor of the fort. Magnolia hopped around and around it, eyeing it suspiciously.

"Do you like it?" asked Nashville. "Do you think I could fit it onto you?"

Magnolia seemed to understand, and stood perfectly still like she was being measured for a suit at the tailor. Nashville slid the strap around her waist and back, and attached it to the base of her unusable wing.

"Go ahead, try it out," Nashville prodded.

Magnolia moved the wing about a bit, but took several tries before the muscle at the base of her old wing adjusted to the new addition. She moved it on its own, then many times in succession with her good wing. She moved them faster and faster, beginning to hop about.

"Not too bad," said Nashville. "Not too bad at all."

Nashville lifted her to the windowsill, thinking she'd be thrilled to get out into the sky and try out the wings.

"Here you go," he said gently, placing her on the ledge.

But Magnolia was not exactly thrilled. Instead, she shuddered and backed away, tweeting and crying out until Nashville helped her back to the floor.

"Hmm," said Nashville. He inspected the wing, looking at it from every angle, checking and double-checking his calculations.

"Magnolia," he said. "We're pretty good friends by now, right? Well, can you just take my word? I promise you this wing will work."

Magnolia looked at him. He was, as usual, having trouble reading her reaction.

"Trust me," said Nashville.

He lifted the tiny bird in his hands and brought her over to the window once again. This time Magnolia did not struggle or strain, she merely kept her eyes on Nashville.

And so, without fanfare or ado, Nashville tossed Magnolia into the air as if he were a parent at the pool teaching his child to swim. Magnolia faltered for a moment, pausing in the air like a cartoon character run off a cliff, but quickly it all came back to her. She flapped once, twice, and suddenly the little bird was flying.

"It worked," said Nashville. "It's actually working!"

The little bird chirped and flew around the pecan tree. So excited was she, so thrilled to be in the air, it seemed she had forgotten all about the injury. Her wings kept on flapping, and Magnolia kept on flying around the tree.

Finally, she stopped and landed on the edge of the window where she and Nashville had sat so many times gazing at the world beyond.

Nashville bowed. He blew Magnolia a kiss.

And the little bird, well, she flew on out into the cinnamon air, so sweet.

After she left, Nashville looked down at the drawings

of the wing he had built. A wing is certainly a powerful thing, but without flight, it loses its magic like a wand without a magician. No Alakazam or Alakazoo. No Bibbidi, Bobbidi, or Boo. *If only*, Nashville thought, staring at his invention. *If only I had wings big enough for me* . . .

THE SINGING TREE

THE DAYS OF FALL STRETCHED ON, AS DID THE afternoons in Miss Starling's classroom at school. Nashville waited each day for the short time after lunch when the class was allowed to get outside the walls of school and into the fresh, clean air.

At the edge of the kickball field stood a tree. It was green and perfect, the lowest branches lining up in a way that seemed custom-made for climbing. And so Nashville did just that. Once he was lost in the foliage, he closed his eyes and imagined he was home, not just at recess, and he didn't have to try to be a regular student when everyone knew he wasn't.

Soon, a little brown bird landed on the branch beside him, and was quickly joined by several others. Not wanting to be rude, Nashville tried to strike up a conversation.

"So," he asked, "do you by any chance know a bird named Magnolia? She was a good friend, and I find it a bit curious that she hasn't written a postcard."

The birds only stared.

"Never mind," Nashville continued. "So, were you originally hatched here, or do you come from someplace else?"

The birds stopped staring and went back to their preening.

"Do you think," Nashville said, continuing his one-way conversation, "that you could fly around the world so fast, you could relive your favorite day? Also, do you think wind is fast-moving air, or something moving *through* air? Also, when you are flying and you have to . . . you know . . . do you ever aim for certain people's heads?"

The birds did not reply. And so, to fill the quiet on the branch between them, Nashville began to whistle.

Whistling. Nashville had always loved this simple

act, and had never taken the value of it for granted. Whistling, like cake, was almost exclusively reserved for times of happiness and relaxation—for drawing joy (and dogs) a little bit closer. One never whistled to deter something or because work was just too hard. No, the whistle was pure sunshine through the lips in every regard.

So on that day, with the birds on his branch, Nashville whistled what he hoped was a joyful tune. To his delight, the birds joined along.

Zay-zay-zay-zoo-zee, sang the first little bird.

Tika-tika-swee-chay-chay, sang the second.

Cheerup-cheerup-cheerily, sang the third

And so, Nashville and the birds found a way to converse.

Zay-zay-zay-zoo-zee

Just some birds singin' in a tree

Tika-tika-swee-chay-chay

Gonna sing all night, sing all day

Cheerup-cheerup-cheerily

Gonna sing far and nearily

Wheet-wheet-wheet-eo

Gonna sing so nice and sweet-eo
Seebit-seebit-see-see-see
Zee-zee-zee-zoo-zee
Chick-chick-chickadee

Nashville thought that if someone heard the birds from outside it would seem, once again, as if a tree were singing. But what would this tree sing about? Perhaps, like most, the tree would sing of the wishes she had trouble putting into words. Maybe the tree dreamed of lifting her roots and dancing. Maybe she dreamed of mossy slippers, and each leaf of her tutu buoying her as she spun in a pirouette. When she finished, she would curtsy to Nashville.

"Thank you," the tree would say.

"Any time," he would reply as the other trees fluttered their leaves in applause.

Nashville's daydream was suddenly shattered when the birds stopped singing and exploded from the tree, leaves and feathers flying. Something had alarmed them. Something had made them flee. When Nashville looked down, he realized he was no longer alone.

A MURDER OF CROWS

BELOW THE TREE STOOD A GROUP OF BOYS from Nashville's class.

"Who are you talking to up there?" asked Finnes Fowl, a freckle-faced boy.

Nashville did not reply, only began climbing down the branches, more deftly and quickly than the other students had ever seen anyone exit a tree.

"Was that your flock?" asked Finnes, the others laughing along.

Nashville reached the ground and stood with his back to the tree.

"Well actually," he said, "not all groups of birds are called flocks. It's a common mistake."

The boys raised their eyebrows in unison at the unexpected reply.

"A flock, a gaggle," continued Nashville. "Those are the words for birds that most folks know. But some are surprising, and pretty perfect. A bouquet of pheasants for example." He paused to think. "Oh yes, a caldron of raptors! That one's swell. A charm of hummingbirds. An exaltation of larks. A parliament of owls." He said each name reverently like a spell. "A murder of crows."

"You're weird," said Finnes loudly when Nashville had finished. The students all looked at one another and laughed nervously. All except one large boy, whose name Nashville did not know.

"Really," asked the large boy with his forehead creased in thought. "Are they really called a *murder* of crows?"

"Yes," said Nashville. "I have a book you could borrow."

The large boy was about to reply when Finnes interrupted and pushed him aside.

"So, do you actually think your parents were birds?"

"I don't think it," replied Nashville. "I know it. I have the egg I hatched from at my house. It's cornflower blue with mahogany spots that look like continents."

"Yuck," said a boy in the back of the group.

"Gross," said another.

"You know what I think?" continued Finnes. "I think you're a liar. I think you're a little lying weirdo and you didn't hatch from no egg, and your parents weren't no dumb birds. These probably aren't even real."

And before Nashville knew what was happening, Finnes pushed him against the tree, pinned his chest, and plucked a feather from his head.

"Ouch," whispered Nashville, rubbing his scalp.

"Whoa," said Finnes backing away, dropping the feather like it was on fire. "You really do have feathers."

The recess bell rang and, after one last look, the other students ran toward the entrance to the school. Nashville hung back for a moment. He considered climbing back up the tree and hiding all day. But finally he sighed, picked up his lost feather from the ground, and made his way back to class.

A GADGET, A GIZMO, AN INVENTION

THE FIRST THOUGHT NASHVILLE HAD AS HE left school that day was a daydream about finding a tree on the playground tall enough to let him hide behind the clouds and avoid the boys at school.

The second thought he had was that it would be better to never go back to school at all.

And the third thought he had was just one word, so lovely he dare not even speak it. Instead, he wrote it on a small slip of paper.

The word was *Wings*.

He stared at it for a while. *Wings.* He imagined the *W* looked like two bird wings itself, and the rest of the word was in flight, singing along behind it. Finally, not knowing what else to do, he folded the paper, went to the library, and handed it to the librarian.

"Hmm," said the old librarian, pushing up her thick glasses. "Wings." She walked slowly, slowly through the stacks, picking books off the shelves and handing them to Nashville.

"Wings," she repeated. "Wings, wings."

Nashville stayed there all morning reading his way down the stack of books. He learned that bird wings evolved in two ways, that preflight birds were hopping a lot, up into the air to catch and grab things, or away from predators. They were also leaping from tree to tree. Eventually, after many, many, many years of all this hopping and leaping, birds were able to fly. But that was just the scientific answer.

The librarian had also given Nashville other books. Prettier books. Books full of poems and feathers.

Nashville only knew he liked the poems. He understood the poems. He loved the sound when he read *Hope is the thing with feathers/That perches in the soul.* And *I too am not a bit tamed—I too am untranslatable; I sound my barbaric yawp over the roofs of the world.* Poetically speaking, Nashville realized, wings started with a *desire.* The pre-wing birds wanted things; they wanted the tops of trees, or the cloudless skies, or the stars. Who could really be sure?

So Nashville figured he was already on his way, since he certainly had the desire to fly, and hope, and somewhere in him a very barbaric yawp. So now all he needed were the actual materials and tools. Using Magnolia's wing for inspiration, Nashville made a trip to the Goosepimple Curiosity Shop on his way home from the library.

"To help you find what you need," said the wart-nosed proprietor, "I need to know what you're building."

"Oh, you know," said Nashville, not wanting to divulge his plan, "a device. A doohickey. A doodad."

"Eh?" said the owner.

"An apparatus, a gadget, a gizmo. A thingamajig. A whatchamacallit."

"Ah," said the owner finally. "An *invention.*"

Like the librarian, the curiosity shop proprietor walked down the aisles of his shop, poking and pulling items off dusty shelves. Nashville followed at a safe distance as the owner handed him various items: an umbrella, a ship sail, shoelaces, and a hat rack made from bamboo. He handed him a teapot, and one captain's wheel. Nashville teetered to the register with the items.

"Perfect," he said. "Just what I was looking for."

BOX OF QUESTIONS,
SUITCASE OF FEATHERS

"So," asked Nashville's father at dinner, "tell us what's been happening at school?"

Nashville was glad when Junebug began prattling about every detail of her day—about the girl with the koala backpack, the pudding fight at lunch, and the freshly painted hopscotch lines on the playground. This gave Nashville time to think of something to say, since he definitely couldn't tell them about the boys on the playground. It was just the kind of thing his mother—or even worse, Junebug—would show up at his school, and make a big stink about.

"And what about you, Nashville?" asked his mother. "Anything fun happening in your class?"

"Well," said Nashville, thinking, "I've been working on this assignment we got."

"Maybe you didn't hear her ask if anything *fun* was happening," said Junebug, crinkling her nose.

"Our teacher," continued Nashville, "Miss Starling, had us each think of a question. And so everyone sat, tapping their feet and pencils, thinking of questions, getting ready to put them into a box. Once they were inside everyone wondered what they said, buzzing there like a box full of bees."

"So what was the assignment?" asked Nashville's father.

"Our assignment," explained Nashville, "is to answer our own question."

"How interesting," said his mother. "And what was your question?"

"My question," said Nashville, "is a secret." He paused. "Well, a secret until I figure out the answer."

"Oh . . ." said his mother. "And? Do you think you'll be able to answer it?" she asked softly.

"Maybe," replied Nashville. "Yes. I think maybe I'll be able to answer it soon."

After dinner, Nashville hurried upstairs to begin work on his wings.

First, he took out his suitcase of feathers. A whole suitcase! Yes, Junebug had proven to be quite the hunter, and Nashville had exchanged nearly his entire piggy bank for the haul of feathers she'd brought him.

Next, he started working on the coat hangers, reshaping the wires until they looked like the skeleton of a bird's wings. He held them against a large, flat piece of leather, and traced the outline. He cut the pieces of leather and some scraps of an old ship's sail into pieces, each fitting into the skeleton, making them resemble bat wings. But they weren't supposed to be bat wings, they were to be bird wings, and for that he'd have to figure out the feathers, and this would be the hardest part.

Feathers, Nashville knew, were more complicated than most folks realized.

"I wonder . . ." Nashville said to the feathers as he emptied the suitcase. "I wonder if you were sad when you fell to the ground. I wonder if you ever thought you'd have a chance to fly again."

ENCHANTED BALLOONS

THE NEXT DAY WAS SATURDAY, SO Nashville rode his bicycle down the hill to what he referred to as his part-time job. This was putting it a bit loftily, since old Mrs. Craw, the tiny but fierce owner of the pet shop, didn't exactly pay him. She did, however, allow him to play with the animals and birds, which she claimed he had "a real way with" due to his "unique" looks. Nashville liked the job and figured it was one place he blended in just fine.

That afternoon, like most afternoons, Mrs. Craw left

Nashville to watch the shop while she went and played canasta.

"You're in charge," she told him as she left. "I have some imperative vocational commerce in town." Mrs. Craw was fond of words that were twice her size.

Nashville liked being alone in the shop. He liked the smell of cedar, and the sound the mice made when they sipped their water bottle. He liked the softness of puppy ears, and the NO FISHING sign in the fish tank. He especially liked the birds—the exotic, bright birds, bopping like jesters in a royal court.

Nashville looked at the birds in their cages, thinking about how odd it must feel to be able to fly, but not allowed. They looked back up at him and seemed to speak with their eyes. The caged birds seemed to all be asking the same exact question.

And their question brought up an idea, an answer, in Nashville.

"It's a bit crazy," he said. "But maybe. Just maybe . . ."

"I think we're ready," announced Nashville two hours later, holding the ends of the strings. "Here goes nothing."

And with that, he flung open the doors to the pet shop. Attached to strings and held by tight knots, the birds flew and spread out. They were like dogs on leashes, except in the sky.

"It's working!" Nashville shouted, dancing below. He looked very much like a salesman holding a colorful bunch of enchanted balloons.

He turned, made sure to be responsible and lock the door to the shop behind him, then let the birds lead the way.

And what joy the birds must have felt, the wind once again running through their feathers. For a moment the strings disappeared, and they were free.

"Now, now," said Nashville. "Be respectful. No tangling, we're not trying to make a maypole here."

One bluebird closed its eyes and imagined dipping down the meadow, past the nest where he had been hatched, the shells now crushed to powder, over the churchyard, straight up, until like rain into a puddle, the bluebird merged with bluest sky.

Nashville took a turn onto the main street of Goosepimple. As he walked, the townsfolk began to take notice and emerge, one by one, from their perfect houses.

"Why I never," a man said as he stood with a hose watering his garden.

"I want one," a little girl said, looking up at her mother.

"Meow," cried a cat, looking hungrily at the birds.

Soon, the entire street was lined with onlookers, and the murmurs and questions danced from freshly cut lawn to freshly cut lawn. Heads started popping out of upstairs windows, and it wasn't long before a reporter for the *Goosepimple Tribune* showed up with his camera.

"Is this some kind of promotional stunt?" he asked, his flashbulbs popping.

"Oh no," said Nashville. "I just feel one should take a stroll on such a fine day, don't you? Even if one happens to be a bird."

He continued past the candy shop and the five-and-dime, where children pressed their faces against the glass. He finally reached the town square, where, storming across the grass, was the squat figure of Mrs. Craw.

"Nashville! What on earth are you doing?"

"I just thought," he said quickly, "that it's such a nice

day with such a warm breeze, perhaps the birds would like to go for a stroll. . . ."

"Have you lost your mind?" Mrs. Craw shouted, trying to untangle the strings. Her face was so red and round, it, too, looked like a balloon ready to pop.

"You . . . you . . ." she was so busy figuring out what to yell, she barely noticed that the birds were dragging her heels off the ground. Yes, for a moment it seemed the wee woman could float away like the basket beneath a hot-air balloon, never to be seen again.

"Nashville!" she shouted as the birds dragged her toward the shop. "Nashville you are absolutely, irrefutably, indubitably *FIRED!*"

FEATHERS DON'T
FIT IN

WHEN NASHVILLE'S FATHER PICKED HIM up outside the pet shop, Nashville was standing with a police officer, a reporter from the *Goosepimple Tribune*, and several of the town's busiest busybodies.

Nashville's father didn't look very happy at all. His brow was furrowed and creased, the way it always became when he didn't know what to say to his son. They walked quietly up the hill to the house in the pecan tree.

"Nashville," he said, finally breaking the silence, "I'm not mad."

"You're not?" asked Nashville.

"No," said his father. "I don't agree with what you did, but I think, on some level, I can understand why you did it."

"I was trying to be a good friend," replied Nashville.

"And that's great," said his father. "A bit ill conceived in this case, but a tip-top quality in anyone. But . . ."

"But?" asked Nashville.

"But I think," said his father, "maybe you could spend less time with your bird friends, and more time with your classmates. Invite them over to play. Go to the field and get some grass stains."

"The other kids don't like me," Nashville said, nearly whispering. "A boy in my class even plucked one of my feathers."

His father stopped walking and knelt down in front of Nashville. He put his hands on his son's shoulders.

"They just don't know you like we do," he said. "They'd like you if they did. All I'm asking," he continued, "is that you give it a chance. I think you'll be surprised how many friends you'd make if you just try to fit in a little bit. Will you do that? For me?"

"Yes," said Nashville. "I can do that. And I think I know just what you mean."

"You'd like *what?*" asked the barber, an ancient old man with the posture of a jumbo shrimp. Nashville sat in the chair at the barbershop. Normally when he went there he simply requested a preen—a few feathers off the top—but this time he had a new request.

"I'd like you to get rid of my feathers," said Nashville.

The barber looked nervous. "You sure?"

"Yes," said Nashville, who didn't seem all that sure. "Cut them. Snip them. Buzz them all off. No more feathers. Feathers don't fit in."

And so, reluctantly, the old man went to work. His scissors clipped and snipped away until the air was full of feathers. The barber's assistant, a young, soundless boy, shuffled around the shop with a broom and dustpan trying to keep up with the storm. Finally, the barber took out his electric razor, and buzzed the last bits of feather from Nashville.

"Ta-da," said the barber, brushing Nashville's neck and shoulders. "You are feather free, my young friend."

When he turned the chair around Nashville gasped—
he had never seen himself without a crown of feathers on
his head, and the sight of his own baldness was alarming.
He ran his hands over the smoothness, and it reminded
him of the way a baby's head looks. It reminded him of
an egg. It reminded him of something he hardly recog-
nized at all.

"How do you like it?" asked the barber.

"Perfect," said Nashville in a small, cracking voice.
"Now I'll fit right in."

WHEN IT RAINS IN GOOSEPIMPLE

T HAT NIGHT IN THE VILLAGE OF GOOSEPIM-
ple it began to rain.

It rained sideways and backward, down, and sometimes it seemed to rain up as well. It rained so long and
so hard that after three days the news began report-
ing there was a chance there would be a flood, the
likes of which Goosepimple had not seen in over ten
years. It rained and rained while Nashville and Junebug
stared out the foggy windows, their board games lying
exhausted on the carpet, their markers dried up from all
work and all play.

Nashville slipped away a few times, opening his toy chest, where he'd stashed the nearly finished wings. He'd worked night after night sewing on each individual feather, and he'd finished attaching the straps that would fit them to his body. He'd finished them except for one thing—one thing was missing, and he wasn't quite sure what it was.

"When will it *stop*?" Junebug asked, staring out the window.

"I don't know," said Nashville. "But it will."

He was right, of course. One day, after a week of storming, the rain stopped falling just as suddenly as it had started.

"See," said Nashville. "No weather lasts forever."

And so Nashville and Junebug put on their galoshes and went out into the world. After so many days of rain, it was cool and cleansed and damp under the pecan tree. Fat water drops fell branch-to-branch, leaf-to-leaf, onto the ground. They fell on Nashville and Junebug, who lay on the ground under the tree, too happy to be outside to care about the wet grass, too excited to see and touch everything as only two children can be after a solid week of rain.

"Hey, Nashville?" said Junebug.

"Yeah?" said her brother.

"Mom and Dad told me not to say anything about it, because you're going through something called 'growing pains.' But I have to tell you . . ." She seemed reluctant to continue in a very un-Junebug-like way. "Well, I preferred you with feathers,"

"Yeah," said Nashville, laughing, the drops from the tree falling on his bare head. "It's been too rainy out for all this fitting in."

They stayed there, watching the raindrops fall down to the ground where they disappeared. But not really, of course, they only vanished to the naked eye. The rain had come, and it had gone, but it would still be there around them; under the ground the roots of the pecan tree would have their share, and the pale threads of the grasses, and the feet of moss. A few drops would enter the mole's tunnel, and eventually, some would even find their way down to stones that, after being buried for thousands of years, would finally be able to feel the sky.

YOU'RE ALL RIGHT

NASHVILLE WORE A HAT TO SCHOOL, BUT as soon as the bell rang, Miss Starling asked him to please take it off. He heard murmers and whispers around the room, but it wasn't until recess, sitting in his tree, that someone said anything to him about his featherless head.

"Hey." It was, to Nashville's surprise and dismay, Finnes Fowl standing below the tree.

The large boy wrapped his large hands around a low branch. After three tries he finally hoisted one leg up as well, then pulled and grunted himself onto the branch.

Nashville scooted aside to avoid being pushed out of the tree, or worse.

"So why'd you do it?" asked Finnes. "It looked less stupid before." He pointed to Nashville's featherless head.

Nashville was shocked. Finnes seemed to be giving him some sort of . . . compliment? Well, almost.

"That's what my sister said, too," replied Nashville. He could hardly believe he was having an actual conversation with Finnes Fowl. He tried to keep it going. "You really liked the feathers better? I thought you thought they were gross or something."

In response the boy pointed to his own leg.

"Wanna see something gross?" he asked.

Nashville looked down to see Finnes's leg, covered in vicious, red spots. It reminded Nashville of the pictures in their science book of the supernova, the dots meshed together in the center, then spreading over his whole leg.

"I've had it since I was born," explained Finnes. "I've never worn short pants before. But then you came to school, looking like you do, and I thought heck, if that pip-squeak can come to school with feathers, maybe I can show my legs. So I asked Ma to take me shopping."

"And you got yourself some shorts?" asked Nashville.

"Yup," said Finnes smiling. "I got myself some shorts. You should have seen it. Ma tried to act like it was no big deal, but then when she thought I wasn't looking, I saw her wipe her eyes."

Finnes swung his legs. He let the bare skin brush against the cool, green leaves on the tree.

"That's good," said Nashville. "This is a nice time of year for shorts."

"Right," laughed Finnes. He rubbed Nashville's head and jumped from the tree with a thud.

"You're all right, little guy." And with that, Finnes Fowl marched away to his friends, leaving Nashville alone and smiling in his tree.

QUESTIONS AND ANSWERS

SOON, IT WAS TIME FOR THE STUDENTS IN Miss Starling's class to present the answers to the questions they had placed in the box like buzzing bees.

The girl with a freckle on every spare bit of skin made her way to the front of the room.

"Go on," prompted Miss Starling. "What was your question?"

The girl turned red, her freckles merging with the rest of her blushing skin.

"My . . . my question was . . ." She stopped. "I don't really think I should read it."

"Why not?" asked Miss Starling.

"Because," the girl said quietly, "it's about someone in our class."

A look of shock swept over Miss Starling's face, but only for the briefest moment. She took a deep breath.

"Go on," she said.

"It was about Nashville," explained the girl. "But that was at the beginning of school, and I'd never seen anyone like him. But now I don't wonder my question anymore. So I picked a new question, one about how flowers grow."

The girl went on to tell the class about water and sunshine and how the plants could grow.

"The earth laughs in flowers," she said, quoting from her paper.

The next to present was a boy with teeth like loose shutters. He explained about gas and matter and hydrogen and space

"When it is dark enough," he finished, "you can finally see the stars."

Miss Starling smiled. "You can take your seat now."

But the boy kept standing.

"That wasn't my real question," he said, looking down at his shoes.

"Oh?" asked Miss Starling.

"Mine was actually about Nashville, too."

"What was it?" asked Nashville. Everyone turned to look at him.

"I wanted to know if you were, like, a *mutant*. Like a superhero, I mean," the boy quickly continued. The class laughed at this.

"And?" asked Miss Starling.

"I guess he is, kind of," said the boy. "But not in the usual way."

The boy sat down. One by one the rest of the class stood and read their questions from the beginning of the school year. Braver now, they looked at Nashville as they read.

What is he?

Why is he?

Was he a mistake?

Almost all the questions, it seemed, had been about Nashville. But his classmate's answers, Nashville realized, were not really about him at all.

"I hate how tall I am," said a girl taller than the boys. "But it's not that big of a deal."

"It's like, who cares if you have a stupid stutter, or feathers, or whatever," said another boy, hardly stuttering at all. "None of that really matters."

"Actually," said the prettiest girl in school, as she focused her eyes right on Nashville, "I wish we all had feathers," she continued. "I think they're beautiful."

Now it was Nashville's turn to blush.

"Nashville," said Miss Starling, interrupting his thoughts. "I believe it's your turn."

Nashville nodded, stood, and slowly made his way to the front of the class. It was the end of the school day, the air warm. But everyone in Miss Starling's room was wide-awake.

Nashville cleared his throat. He did not have a paper to read from, and instead spoke while looking out at the class.

"My question," he said, "is *why can't I fly?*"

"And?" said Miss Starling. "What is your answer?"

"I don't have one," answered Nashville.

"Why not?" asked Miss Starling.

"Because," said Nashville. He stopped then, looked at his class, the one he'd found so scary at the beginning of the year. The ones that now made him brave with their kind words.

"Because," he said, "I think I *can*."

WHO'S NEXT?

THE CLASS SAT VERY STILL AFTER NASH-
ville's statement, and for what seemed like an eter-
nity, didn't make a sound. And then, finally, the silence
was broken by none other than Finnes Fowl.

"Prove it," said Finnes, with more joy than mocking
in his voice. "If you can fly, then prove it."

"Okay," replied Nashville. "I will."

And with that statement, Nashville smiled a giant-
sized smile, turned, and ran out the door of the
schoolhouse.

"Nashville!" yelled Miss Starling. "Stop! Come back
here! Where are you going?"

But Nashville did not stop.

He hooted. He hollered. He sounded what could only be called a barbaric yawp.

Nashville ran and ran and ran all the way into the village of Goosepimple. He ran through his favorite park, and around his favorite tree; he waved to the puppets in the puppet shop, the old men gossiping on their porches, and several barking dogs.

He was, in his own way, saying good-bye to Goosepimple.

The last place he stopped was the pet shop. A closed sign hung on the door—likely due to Miss Craw playing canasta—but through the windows he could see the cages hanging around the store, birds hopping from perch to perch, or tossing around seeds, or staring at themselves in the mirror thinking they had a friend.

And then, all of a sudden, he knew exactly what to do. He found himself doing something that, until that day, he would have thought impossible.

Nashville broke into the pet shop.

It wasn't very hard actually. Nobody in Goosepimple

locked their doors, and even when they did, they hid the key somewhere close. Nashville knew the key to the pet shop was under a stone turtle by the door.

The birds started squawking their alarm the minute he walked inside.

"Keep it down," he said. "You can yell all you want once you're out."

First Nashville propped the front door wide open. Next he flung open the large windows to the shop. And then, one by one, he unlocked every birdcage in the store. He stood back, waiting for them all to burst forward, but to his astonishment, not one of them moved.

"Haven't you ever heard the saying free as a bird?" he asked. "What are you waiting for?"

Finally, a small lovebird hopped onto the edge of her cage door.

"That's it. Go on," Nashville whispered. "Be brave. Be bold."

The lovebird puffed her chest once as if making a final decision, then flew out of her cage and out the door of the shop.

"Woohoo!" shouted Nashville.

The birds tilted their heads to the side. What a peculiar thing had just occurred.

"Who's next?" asked Nashville.

The lovebird's mate, not wanting to be alone, was the next to leave his cage.

"Good choice," encouraged Nashville. "Bravo."

It must be true what they say, because those birds of a feather began flocking together, right out the door to the shop. It all happened in one great whoosh! It was like a tornado, the whirlwind of birds and wings and feathers that rushed out the door and window, Nashville in the center of it all, spinning, arms up, yelling like madman.

He followed them, still hooting and hollering, out the door to the shop. He watched them get smaller and smaller as they flew away, like a bunch of balloons accidentally—or in this case quite on purpose—released. He made a mental note to leave instructions on his piggy bank, a note saying that its contents should be paid to Miss Craw for the birds.

"I'm coming, too!" shouted Nashville after the birds. "I'll be right behind you!"

THE FINAL FEATHER

W HEN NASHVILLE ARRIVED HOME, HE could hear his parents once again talking in the kitchen. The phone was ringing over and over, and when his father answered, Nashville heard words like *expulsion* and *school grounds*. Words like *break-in* and *pet shop*. After his father hung up the phone, Nashville heard more clips of conversation. He knew what they were discussing, and he crept around behind the pecan tree to avoid it.

But when Nashville rounded to corner, he found

himself face-to-face with Junebug climbing down the ladder to the fort.

"What are you doing?" asked Nashville.

Junebug smiled her biggest, goofiest smile at Nashville.

"I found your wings," she said. "They're amazing."

"Wh-what?" asked Nashville. He wasn't sure what to say.

"Or," Junebug continued, "I should say they were almost amazing."

"No," Nashville said, climbing up the tree so fast his foot slipped twice and he nearly fell. "What did you do to them?"

When he reached the fort, he saw the wings there, perfect and intact, not decorated with sparkles or glitter or any of the other Junebug crafting fears that had flashed through his mind.

"They're done," said Nashville in awe. He wasn't quite sure why, but the wings seemed like they were perfect.

"But what did you do?" he asked.

"Everyone's looking for you," Junebug replied.

"But what did you *do*?" Nashville asked again.

"I know you have to leave," said Junebug. "I know, and it's okay. I won't tell them to come up until you're ready to go."

"But . . ."

"I added the last feather," said Junebug. "This one." She pointed to a perfect feather at the tip of the wing, one that made it all come together.

"This one," she smiled, "is the one I found after that rainstorm. I looked it up, and wouldn't you know it— this lucky feather came from the wing of a Nashville warbler."

A FAREWELL CAKE

NASHVILLE STAYED IN THE FORT AND GOT things organized while Junebug went downstairs.

"He's in his fort," Junebug told her parents. "But he really wants to be alone for a little while."

"I'm worried," said his mother, her face washed in a rainy-day light. "I wish things were easier for him."

"I know what we should do," chimed Junebug. "We should make him a cake. Just like you did when he was being stubborn and wouldn't hatch from his egg."

"A cake," said her mother. She gave Junebug a knowing look. "Now that just might work."

"But he's in big trouble," protested Nashville's father. "He ran from school. He freed all the birds in town!"

But one look from his wife and daughter, and he went to fetch the mixing bowl. They put in the ingredients—eggs and flour and sugar—and Junebug stirred with ancient eggbeaters. She held out the bowl of batter to her father.

"Put something in," she told him.

"Pardon?"

"It's a Nashville cake, so you need to put in some Nashville. Watch, I'll show you." She held up an imaginary container and turned it over the bowl, pretending to shake the contents into the mix. "I'm pouring in one box of the feathers on his head, looking silly when he comes down for breakfast."

"And I," said her mother pretending to pour, "am putting in a dollop of the way he sings made-up songs when he thinks no one is listening."

"His wonderful taste in hats," added Junebug. "His sense of direction."

They put in every hum and every hiccup; every sun and cloud that had passed across his face; every lovely thing that they loved about Nashville and some, in truth, that they had failed to appreciate, as well.

"I put in every feather," added his father quietly. "I hope he can forgive me someday for telling him to fit in."

They also remembered to add some real sugar, and butter, and flour, and when the batter was finally done, they poured it into the baking pans, opened the oven door, and put everything inside to bake. Slowly the ingredients started to mix, the kitchen and house filling with the delicious smell of cake.

SEND ME POSTCARDS

WHEN THE CAKE WAS FINISHED, JUNEBUG took her mother's and father's hands and brought them to the very top floor of the house—to the dazzling, oversized window. The window his mother had sat at ten years earlier singing, wishing, and waiting for a cornflower-blue egg to hatch.

And there stood Nashville, wearing his homemade wings.

"Oh," said his father.

"My baby," said his mother.

Nashville's parents did not have much more to say.

They knew without words, (in that way parents always seem to know), what Nashville had already decided. Perhaps they had always known—having in their own way willed Nashville into the world—that he could not stay. Perhaps they knew better than other folks that some things are too extraordinary to stay in our world for very long, and so the time they are here should be taken as a gift, as a pause for a moment in front of us, as a hummingbird at the bell of a flower.

"Do you have your good scarf?" asked his father, his hands shaking ever so slightly as he hugged his son and touched his wings. "And your long underwear?" he continued, standing back and looking at his son. "Perhaps you should bring an extra pair of socks. Weather can be . . . very unpredictable."

"Oh, I almost forgot," cried his mother. "We baked you a cake."

There, in her arms, was the finished cake, expertly decorated by his family. It was Nashville all right—same smile. But there was something extra as well. There, frosted and attached to each side of the cake, were wings—two beautiful, beautiful wings.

"Thank you," he said to his family. "It's the perfect cake."

"It was Junebug's idea," they explained.

Nashville's father held his mother as she dabbed her eyes with a handkerchief, and watched Junebug walk her big brother to the window.

The wind blew and the white buds danced outside. Junebug looked at Nashville, and then at the window. She imagined him flying away, farther and farther, his shadow lengthening over the endless ground, until he was just a speck of white and gold wings in the distant sky.

"Will you write me?" she asked.

"I'll send you postcards," said Nashville. "I'll send them on the wind."

And then, as strangely as he'd come into their world, Nashville spread his wings and flew away from his mother, father, and sister; he flew away from the house in the pecan tree into the cinnamon air, so sweet.

THE LEAP

A ND SO, WITH THE FIRST GOLDEN GLOW OF sunlight rising over the hills, Nashville glided to a distant treetop. There, in the pine bough, he was out of sight of his family, and able to gather his thoughts.

"On the one hand," Nashville said to himself, "I'll start really flying. Not just floating, but also flapping. On the other hand . . ."

If a scientist could have taken a microscopic cross-section of Nashville's heart at that moment, this is what they would have seen: a map of the sky. A map that had been folded and refolded too many times, like an overdreamed dream, the crease lines becoming soft and fuzzy. The arrow on the map's compass only pointed one way, and that way was the sky.

"Be brave," Nashville said to himself. "Be brave."

And then, to his surprise and delight, he glided on an updraft high, high into the sky.

"I'm doing it," he said, quite shocked. "I'm really flying."

He continued to glide, over the hill and pecan tree, circling like a bird, like a moon orbiting the only home he'd ever known.

A lullaby of clouds encircled Nashville and floated him like a ball across the syllables of a sing-along song in the sky. He tried to think how he'd describe it all to Junebug—piercing the wind and touching nothing but air was like swimming, but not quite. Like freefalling on a roller coaster. But not quite.

Nashville finally began to flap the wings, and that worked as well. He changed direction, and flew over the entire town.

Nashville circled the school, but the school yard was quiet and empty, and he knew they would all be having reading lessons that time of day. He saw all the balls, Frisbees, and toys on the roof. He dipped low, kicking the balls and throwing toys down to the ground, wondering what all his classmates would think if they could see him now. He pictured Miss Starling's smile, and his whole class whooping and clapping for him. He pictured Finnes Fowl in his shorts, shouting "Way to go, little guy."

Nashville felt it all—the singing of the seasons, the warmth of wind, the sailing of ships, the migration of birds, and the simple, perfect smell of the ground after rain. He felt that there was nothing under his skin but light, and were he to ever fall to the ground, he would merely shine.

He felt all these wonderful things until he heard the worst sound—the sound of something breaking.

THE FALL

NASHVILLE HEARD THE SNAP, FOLLOWED by a rip, followed by the feeling of the wings slipping, falling from his body. The wings first broke along the main support—a loud cracking sound like a bone. Next, the smaller pieces of wood all began to shatter, and this sounded more like branches being stepped on in the forest.

When the wings had broken in enough places, the leather material and feathers began folding and buckling like a collapsing umbrella. This meant that Nashville began to fall, hard and fast, the wind whipping against his face.

He was falling, but Nashville did not scream or cry. He knew he would hit the ground, that's how gravity works. But before that could occur, something very strange, and very lovely, appeared to him.

Now, it is worth noting all the things that did not appear. All the things he did not see or hear or recall as he fell.

Nashville did not see the light inside his egg, how dark it was, how the shadows danced, or the sound of his mother's voice singing.

Nashville did not see geese flying south for winter overhead, or catch a glimpse of their perfect V shape.

He did not recall Magnolia, the soft down of her stomach feathers, or how fast her heart beat when he held her.

Nor did he hear the sound of the countless people who had pointed and laughed at him over his ten short years.

He did not see the sky the color of spider tents, or feel the evening as cold as fish scales, or marvel at the sunset glowing like the inside of a ripe plum.

He did not recall his father teaching him to throw a punch, just in case.

He did not remember dusk. A meadow. Long grass, the first buzzes and hums of night insects all around him as he lay on the damp earth with Junebug by his side. He was not covered with vines that had grown so fast, twisting up, diving in and out of each button-hole on his vest.

He did not see artichokes or blowfish or the purple sunset or the frill-necked lizard. He did not see spiderwebs or eclipses or a star-nosed mole. He saw absolutely no platypuses at all.

This is what he noticed:

As he fell, for one simple, splendid, golden moment, he felt nothing but gratitude; gratitude for his old soul and true heart, for his strange looks and strange beginnings, for all the things that made him Nashville. And the moment this feeling flowed through him, something inside him started to blossom. This great leap began to bring about a great change, and Nashville was finally ready to let it transform him.

WAKE UP, JUNEBUG

"Junebug," whispered Nashville. He stood over his sister in her bed, the night-light's glow beginning to blend into the dawn.

"Junebug, wake up," Nashville said, shaking her small shoulder. Junebug stirred, and then opened her eyes. She looked up at her brother. There, in the first light, Junebug smiled at the sight of Nashville.

"You came back," she said, slowly waking. She put her toes on the cold wood floor, and tiptoed around Nashville.

"The wings," she said, walking around him. "They're different. Did you add feathers? Are they bigger?

They're magnificent, Nashville, like angel wings," gushed Junebug. "They're like nothing I've ever seen."

Slowly, slowly, Nashville began flexing his shoulder muscles.

Slowly, slowly, the wings began to unfold. After a few moments, Nashville was able to extend them both fully.

"They're so beautiful," said Junebug. She inspected them closely, looking at how each feather overlapped perfectly, colored white and brown and gold. "I . . . I just can't believe these are the same wings you built. They are, aren't they?"

Nashville just smiled, and looked to the corner of the room. Junebug followed his gaze into the shadows where something lay against the wall—large and slumped over, shrouded in darkness. Junebug crept closer, closer. Suddenly the truth swept in like the most wonderful breeze.

Junebug smiled.

And she cried.

There in the corner, broken apart and sad, were the remnants of the wings Nashville had built.

BEYOND THE LAUGHING SKY

"THEY'RE REAL," WHISPERED JUNEBUG. "But how?"

"I think . . ." Nashville said with a smile. "I think I had them all along."

Then he took his sister's hand, and led her to the top floor of the house, to the edge of the dazzling, oversized window.

And there, like Peter and Wendy, they stepped out of the window, and up into the never-never land of the air. Junebug clung to her brother at first, but after a few moments she was so entranced by what she saw, she forgot to be afraid at all.

Nashville and Junebug looked below them, and felt the power of seeing a world so familiar from a new, more distant perspective. They flew over the fields where they had run together, and the streams where they had fished and caught frogs. They flew over games they had played, and songs they had sung, marshmallows they had roasted, and sand castles they had built and destroyed. They flew over stacks of books they had read together, and lightning bugs they had caught together; over piles of leaves, and piles of pancakes. They flew over memories of all the years, all the days that seemed so different, but so perfect, when seen from a distance.

Now, here they were flying through chimney smoke and rain-heavy clouds. They flew lower, skimming the tops of houses, and from this place, Nashville and Junebug were able to hear the singing of the trees.

The trees sang of all the things they protected from the cold—of the bluebirds bundled inside together for warmth, and of the hollow nooks where squirrels slept, dreaming, their minds a map of nuts hidden like buried treasure.

They sang songs that tasted of apple pie, of plums and peaches and lemonade grown on the trees. They sang of their grand outfits of moss and mushrooms growing wild. They sang of the rich, dark dirt where the worms and the moles tickled their roots.

They sang of all the trees to go before them and be made into homes and boats, their wood used to make chapels, and doors, and cradles.

But mostly, they sang of a fort in a tree where a boy and a girl would go on grand adventures; they sang of the children swinging, climbing, playing, and building crowns from their leaves. The trees sang softly and sweetly about their branches always being open to little birds. Nashville and Junebug knew the only way was to sing along, and so they joined in with the trees, floating all together for just a little while above the whole, dazzling world.

And what about that world? For Nashville and Junebug were not the only ones awake in Goosepimple.

"Mama. Mama, wake up!" It was a boy standing by his mother's bed.

His mother rubbed the sleep from her eyes, put on a robe, and followed her son. She looked out the window. She rubbed her eyes again.

"Well I never . . ." She ran to the hall, picked up the phone, and called across the street to Mrs. Craw, and Mrs. Craw looked out the window as well.

"Impossible!" cried Mrs. Craw. She picked up the phone and called Dr. Larkin. Dr. Larkin called Miss Starling. And so on and so on, until every woman in curlers and man in slippers were looking up at the sky to get a glimpse of Nashville and Junebug; to hear the faintest, distant, sweet sound of laughter in the sky.

"Impossible," they all said, though the word didn't have quite the huff and puff that it used to.

A SONG TO SING
YOU HOME

THE MORNING WAS THE COLOR OF PALE
blue eggshells, the golden yolk of the sun rising in
the east. Nashville and Junebug flew low to the ground,
where they could hear the last cricket songs of dawn,
where they could see their shadows fly along beneath
them, the shadows of a boy and girl running along
below them, playing and whispering to one another in
the long grass. The air was cool—it whipped their hair
back and reddened their cheeks. Nashville tried to press
the moment into his memory—tried to find a place

he could keep it safe and take it out when he needed it, maybe in the cotton depths of a pocket, or the snap of a locket, or the bottom of a dark trunk. Couldn't he keep all this there—the closeness of clouds, the rooftops and trees like toys below, his sister by his side? He didn't know.

When they returned to the house, they sat on a branch and watched the sun finish rising.

"You could take me with you," Junebug finally said.

"I can't do that," Nashville replied sadly. "Not in a really real way, you know that. You need to stay here."

Junebug thought about this for a moment. There'd be nobody to play with in the fort, and the maps they'd made would yellow and curl with age. Maybe eventually they would replace his nest with a bed or a cradle, the perches with sturdy, normal chairs.

One day, not long from then, Junebug would ask her father, "Where do you think he is now?" And so her parents would take out the globe, and point to a magical place far, far away. And they'd smile, and they'd imagine Nashville flying, soaring, gliding, and seeing the world over the pines. They'd imagine him free.

But for this last moment, her brother was still there.

So Junebug tilted her head to the side as if to listen to the softest music.

"Hey," she asked. "Do you hear that?"

Nashville listened as well. He listened with his whole self, and finally he did hear it. It was the song of a tree. But this one was different—more like it came from inside his own throat, for it was the pecan tree he'd lived in singing, and it was singing a song just for him.

"I do," he smiled. "I do hear it."

Nashville knew that it was time for him to fly away, but no matter where he went, there would always be this: a whisper, a hum, a lullaby. A song singing out over the pines; through the clouds, the lonely hours, and over the rooftops of the world. A song hatched from an egg. A song to sing him home.

THE END OF SPRING

THE HOUSE WAS QUIETER WITHOUT Nashville.

Well, not *quieter* really, but there seemed to be less of *something*. Junebug felt it, but couldn't put it into words. It was as if some magic had been peeled away like wallpaper.

Perhaps it was because when she looked out the window, Junebug still saw Nashville's birdbath covered in green moss and crawling ivy. Perhaps it was the dust gathering on his bureau and his tin soldier toys. And perhaps, just maybe, it seemed something was missing because someone was; Nashville had been gone for most of the spring, the world turning green, smelling of rainstorms and frogs.

Junebug grew accustomed to this new, quieter house, though odd thoughts did sneak up on her from time to time, the main one being just this: How could she have known? How was she to have known that the last time she saw her brother come downstairs for breakfast with his feathers a mess would be the *last* time? The last card game, the last adventure, the last thumb-fight over the first slice of cake. You rarely know, in the moment, when it's the last time you'll do something. Most of the time, the whole thing just sneaks away in the night, never to be seen or heard from again, not even sending back so much as a postcard to say hello.

Oh, there were stories of course, about where Nashville had gone. People claimed to see him just about everywhere, doing just about anything. Some said he'd joined the circus, made friends with the man with webbed feet and the yak girl with horns. Some said they saw him hopping trains like a hobo. Some said he'd never existed at all.

But who would ever *really* know what had become of Nashville?

Junebug would, that's who.

It happened at the end of spring, when the trees had turned from newborn lime to emerald and bottle green. The blossoms were in full bloom. Junebug awoke as always—tangled in her sheets, rubbing sleep from her eyes, rolling over to look out the window and see if there was anything new in the world. There never was. Until, that is, the day the honeysuckle arrived.

It was just a small yellow-orange blossom, nothing too exciting or unusual. What was strange was *how* it was placed, ever so carefully on the edge of her sill. It hadn't blown there, hadn't crept up the wall on its own. The closest honeysuckle bush was at the bottom of the hill, behind the high, high fence.

It could only, she thought, have been flown here.

"Nashville?" she said, though she already knew the answer.

Junebug never told anyone about that honeysuckle that appeared many times at her window that spring. She never told anyone about the bird she would catch

glimpses of from time to time, the one that felt so familiar, the one that would appear at the edge of her vision,
but be gone by the time she turned her head. She never
told anyone that she knew it was Nashville—knew
without a doubt that it was her brother, *her brother*, who
had been granted the power to transform into what he
was always meant to be.

CODA

IMPOSSIBLE

T HERE IS A HOUSE. IT SITS PERCHED IN THE branches of the largest pecan tree in the village of Goosepimple. The tree grows on the top of a high hill, and the hill overlooks a small, perfect village, where the sun always shines, the grass is always mowed, and nobody ever, ever, *ever* uses the word impossible.

It's not a law. It's not patrolled or policed. It's just that everyone in Goosepimple remembers that day, much like any other, when the old men gossiping on their porch looked up, up, up to the sky.

"Why, it looks like an angel in an updraft."

"Naw, it looks like some sort of giant bird."

"Naw," said the third old man. "It looks like . . . *Nash-ville*."

Oh, there were tourists just passing through of course, those who stopped in to ask the old widow who worked in the visitor center.

"Is it true?" they asked. "Did a boy in this town grow wings? Did he really fly?"

"Oh, yes," the widow would say. "Nashville grew wings. Nashville could fly."

"Fiddlesticks," a Southern gentleman would say to the widow. "Folks can't fly. That's impossible."

"What an absurd little word," the widow would reply.

"Pardon?"

"You said impossible," the widow would point out. "There ain't no such thing. There's things you've seen and things you may not have, but there ain't nothing that's impossible, sugar."

ACKNOWLEDGMENTS

I am grateful to Brenda Bowen for believing first; Jake Currie for always reading; Nathan Winstanley for always listening; Zach Robbins for laughing with me; Lola Cuevas, Ray Cuevas, Sheryl Bercier, and Rita DeVarennes for cheering; Sarah Wartell for reminding me to see things more beautifully; Carlyle Massey for promising it would get better; Mary and Edward Rossi for a room with a writing desk; Massachusetts Audubon for allowing me to hold a bird to my ear and listen to its heart. And to Nancy Conescu: You believed in Nashville from the very first day he was hatched.

Thank you, thank you, thank you.

TURN THE PAGE FOR A PREVIEW OF
MICHELLE CUEVAS'S NEXT WHIMSICAL STORY

Chapter One
EVERYONE HATES JACQUES PAPIER

Yes, world, I am writing my memoir, and I have titled the first chapter simply this:

EVERYONE HATES JACQUES PAPIER

I think it captures the exact drama of my first eight years in the world rather poetically. Soon I'll move on to chapter two. This is where I'll confess that the first chapter was, in fact, the truth stretched, much like the accordion body of my wiener dog, François. The stretch would be the word *everyone*. There are three exceptions to this word. They are:

My mother.

My father.

My twin sister, Fleur.

If you are observant, you'll notice that I *did not* include François the wiener dog on this list.

Chapter Two
FRANÇOIS THE EVIL WIENER DOG

A boy and his dog are, quite possibly, the most classic of all classic duos.

Like peanut butter and jelly.

Like a left and right foot.

Like salt and pepper.

And yet.

My relationship with François more closely resembles peanut butter on a knuckle sandwich. A left foot in a bear trap. Salt and a fresh paper cut. You get the picture.

In the interest of truth, it is not entirely François's fault; the cards of life have been stacked rather steeply against him. For starters, I do not believe the person in charge of making dogs was paying attention when they attached François's stumpy legs to his banana-shaped body. Perhaps we'd all be

2

ill-tempered if our stomachs cleaned the floor whenever we went for a walk.

The day we brought him home as a puppy, François sniffed my sister and grinned. He sniffed me and began barking—a barking that has never ceased in the eight years I've been within range of his villainous nose.

Chapter Three
PAPIER'S PUPPETS

It is true that *Papier* is the French word for paper. However, my family does not make or sell paper. No, my family is in the imagination business.

"Are there really that many people who need puppets?" Fleur asked our father. To be honest, I had often wondered the very same thing about our parents' puppet shop.

"Dear girl," our father answered. "I think the real question is, who *doesn't* need a puppet?"

"Florists," Fleur answered. "Musicians. Chefs. Newscasters . . ."

"Oh hello," Father said. "I'm a florist. They say talking to plants helps them grow, and now the puppet and I are chatting and our flowers are thriving." He spun around. "Why, look at me, the piano player, with a puppet on each hand, so now I have four arms instead of just two. I'm a chef, but instead of an oven mitt, I have a puppet to pretend with. Oh look, I'm a newscaster who once delivered the news alone, but now have a puppet for witty banter."

"Fine," Fleur said. "Lonely people without anyone to talk to need puppets. Luckily Jacques and I have each other, and we are going outside to play."

I smiled, waved to our father, and followed Fleur out the door. The bell rang as we left the cool gaze of puppets and greeted the sunshine, winking at us through afternoon clouds.

Chapter Four
NO, REALLY.
EVERYONE HATES JACQUES PAPIER.

School. Who thought of this cruel place? Perhaps it is the same person who matches together the various pieces of wiener dogs. School is a great example of a place where everyone (and I mean *everyone*) hates me. Allow me to illustrate with examples from this very week:

On Monday, our class played kickball. The captains chose players for their team one by one. When they got to me, they just went and started the game. I wasn't picked last; I wasn't picked at all.

On Tuesday, I was the only person who knew the capital of Idaho. I had my arm in the air, even waving it around like a hand puppet on the high sea. But the teacher just said, "Really? Nobody knows the answer? *Nobody?*"

On Wednesday, at lunch, a very husky boy nearly sat on me, and I had to scramble from my seat to avoid certain death.

On Thursday, I waited in line for the bus, and before I could get on, the driver shut the door. Right in my face. "Oh, COME ON!" I shouted, but the words disappeared in a cloud of exhaust. Fleur made the driver stop, got off, and walked home beside me.

And so, on Friday morning, I begged my parents to let me stay home from school. They didn't even say no. They just gave me the silent treatment.

Chapter Five
THE MAP OF US

For as long as I could remember, Fleur and I had been making The Map of Us. There were the easy to draw places: the frog pond, the field with the best fireflies, and the tree where we'd carved our initials in the trunk.

And there were the permanent fixtures in our world as well, like Puppet Shop Peak, the Fjords of François, and the Mountaintop of Mom & Dad.

But then there were the other places.

The best places.

The places that could only be found by us.

There was the stream full of tears that Fleur cried when a boy at school made fun of her teeth. The spot where we buried a time capsule. And the spot where we dug up a time capsule. And the much better place where the time capsule currently resides (for now). There was the sidewalk chalk art gallery we commission each summer. And the tree where I broke the climbing record, and also fell, but we didn't tell Mom and Dad. There was the place where the flamingoose, the bighornbear, and the ostrimpanzee roam and graze. And the knothole in the oak where I kept Fleur's smile, the one she does with her eyes instead of her mouth. There were hiding places, and finding places, and deep wells full of secrets.

Yes, like any best friends, there was a whole world that could only be seen by her and me.

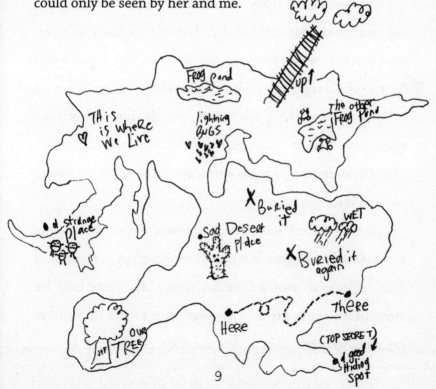

Chapter Six
MAURICE THE MAGNIFICENT

Sometimes, on Sundays, our family would go to the local kids'
museum, which was really just a bunch of bubble blowing, and
old rocks, and baby stuff like that. But that's not why we went.
We went because on Sundays you could get free popcorn and
"enjoy" the "magic" of Maurice the Magnificent.

Maurice was old. I don't mean grandparent old or even
great-grandparent old. I mean *old*. Old like the candles on his
birthday cake cost more than the cake. Old like his memories
were in black and white.

And his tricks! They were the worst. He did one where
he made a dove appear out of a phonograph. A phonograph!
This guy was at least a thousand years old. Every time we
went to his show, Fleur would lean over so I could whisper
my witty remarks.

"Maurice is so old," I whispered, "his report card was written in hieroglyphics."

Fleur covered her mouth with her hands to contain her giggles.

"He's so old," I continued, "that when he was born, the Dead Sea was just coming down with a cough."

Sadly, on that particular Sunday, neither of us noticed that Maurice the Magnificent had noticed *us* mocking his show.

"Little girl," said Maurice, pausing in front of us with a morose rabbit in his hands. "To whom are you whispering?"

"This is my brother," said Fleur. "His name is Jacques."

"Ah," said Maurice, nodding. "And what did *Jacques* say that was so very humorous?"

Fleur's cheeks turned red like her hair, and she bit her lip with embarrassment.

"Well," said Fleur. "He thinks you're . . . old. Oh, and a phony. Jacques said that none of this is real."

"I see," said Maurice. "Well, the world is full of people who will doubt."

Maurice tried to swish his cape with a flourish, hurt his back, and feebly made his way across the stage using his cane.

11

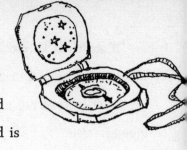

"Doubters will say that magic is only make-believe. And you know what? You don't need to say a word to prove them wrong. All you need is this."

Maurice pulled an old broken compass from his vest pocket. It looked about as old as him, and the arrow only pointed one way: directly at the person holding it.

"Come up here, little girl. You will be my assistant."

Fleur stood, and reluctantly joined Maurice on stage. I felt a twinge of guilt, and hoped he wouldn't put her in a box and stick her with swords.

"Take this," said Maurice. He handed Fleur the compass.

"I'm going to make you disappear," said Maurice. He went over to a person-sized cabinet, opened the door, and motioned for Fleur to step inside. She did, and he closed the cabinet behind her.

"Alakazam!" shouted Maurice. I couldn't help but roll my eyes.

But then, to my utter shock, Maurice opened the cabinet and Fleur was gone! An excited murmur went through the crowd.

"Now, Fleur," hollered Maurice. "If you tap your compass three times, you can come back home."

Maurice closed the cabinet, waited for three taps, and when he opened the door, *POOF!* There was Fleur.

Well, obviously the audience went wild, and old Maurice took a bow (or not; it was hard to tell since his posture was already so stooped). Fleur tried to give back the compass, but Maurice shook his head and folded Fleur's hand over it.

"The world is a mystery with a capital *M*," said Maurice. "The impossible is possible. And you, Fleur, seem like the kind of girl who knows that *real* is merely in the eye of the beholder."

Chapter Seven
FLABBERGASTED

The next day I was fiddling with the compass from the magic show, attempting to make François the wiener dog disappear, when I heard my parents enter their room. The walls in the Papier household are paper-thin, which is how I overheard the conversation that changed the course of my life.

"Do you think," I heard my mother say, "there is such a thing as *too much* imagination?"

"Perhaps," my father replied. "Maybe it was wrong to raise her around so many puppets. Maybe all those googly eyes and moving mouths confused her."

I heard my mother sigh. "And we shouldn't have played along for such a long time. The bunk beds were one thing, but setting an extra place at the table? An extra toothbrush? Buying a second set of books for school? I guess I just

thought Fleur would eventually grow out of having an imaginary friend on her own."

I was shocked.

I was dumbfounded.

I was flabbergasted.

My sister, my sidekick, had an imaginary friend that
she'd never told me about.

Chapter Eight
KNOWN

Oh, Fleur!

We shared everything: bunk beds, baths, banana splits. And don't even get me started on subsequent letters of the alphabet. Once we even shared—brace yourself—a piece of chewing gum. She was chewing, and I had none, and she split it in two like the King Solomon of sweets. Maybe it was yucky. Maybe it was love. And maybe it was a sticky blob of both.

And now a secret as monumental as an imaginary friend?

We were so close. Fleur could read my mind. She knew what I was thinking before I did.

"What would you like for breakfast?" our mother would ask.

And Fleur would shout back, "Jacques wants a pancake

shaped like Mozart's Symphony No. 40! In G minor!"

The weirdest part? I did want that. I *did*.

The truth is, that's all anyone wants, to be known that way, to be seen. I don't mean our hair or our clothes, I mean *seen* for who we really are. We all want to find that one person who knows the real us, all our quirks, and still understands. Have you ever had anyone see you? Really, truly, the deepest part that seems invisible to the rest of the world?

I hope you have.

I have.

I have always had Fleur.